MIRAGE

Newman rolled Oz onto his back and shook the pilot's shoulders. "Captain!" he called.

There was no response.

Feeling a court marshal coming on, the airman slapped Oz's face. "Captain, wake up. We've got trouble."

Oz's eyes fluttered open. "What the hell. . ." he mumbled.

"You've got to wake up, sir . . . Keep your eyes open!"

"Where are we?" Oz asked lethargically, trying to sit up but failing. He looked around dazedly and then tried to focus on Newman.

"Everybody's been drugged or something, sir."

Oz tried to stay awake. "Where's the prince?" he whispered.

**HarperPaperbacks by
Duncan Long**

NIGHT STALKERS
GRIM REAPER
TWILIGHT JUSTICE

Night STALKERS
DESERT WIND

DUNCAN LONG

HarperPaperbacks
A Division of HarperCollins Publishers

This is a work of fiction. The characters, incidents, and
dialogues are products of the author's imagination and are
not to be construed as real. Any resemblance to actual
events or persons, living or dead, is entirely coincidental.

HarperPaperbacks   *A Division of* HarperCollins*Publishers*
                10 East 53rd Street, New York, N.Y. 10022

Copyright © 1991 by Duncan Long
All rights reserved. No part of this book may be used or
reproduced in any manner whatsoever without written
permission of the publisher, except in the case of brief
quotations embodied in critical articles and reviews.
For information address HarperCollins*Publishers*,
10 East 53rd Street, New York, N.Y. 10022.

Cover art by Edwin Herder

First printing: January 1991

Printed in the United States of America

HarperPaperbacks and colophon are trademarks
of HarperCollins*Publishers*

10 9 8 7 6 5 4 3 2 1

For Randy, Kathy, Joshua, Colleen, and Coushatta

ACKNOWLEDGMENTS

I must once again extend my gratitude to Ethan Ellenberg who came up with the basic idea, plot, and locale for this story. Thanks should go to my editors, Ed Breslin and Jessica Kovar, along with the staff at HarperCollins, who have made another Night Stalkers book possible.

Kristen and Nicholas have patiently waited. And special thanks must go to Maggie who helped in everything from chasing down background material to improving plot devices and catching the many typos and mistakes that crept into the first drafts of this manuscript.

Majid Qaim surreptitiously eyed the Beretta Model 12 submachine guns held by the guards. The flickering light of the oil lamps glinted from the blued steel of the firearms.

Qaim remained kneeling on the floor, painfully aware of the hard tiles. He spoke again in *al-lugha al-'ammiyya,* using the Arabic dialect of his tribe. "Kidnapping the prince is a very dangerous undertaking," he asserted. "Are you sure . . ."

"Of course I'm sure, you shifty-eyed louse," bellowed the man sitting on the dais. He jumped to his feet with an oath, pulling his loose-fitting *djellaba* around himself. The chill desert air had seeped through the iron and wooden doors into the low-ceilinged chamber.

Qaim studied his angry client through eyes that were slits. The voice coming through the *keffiyeh* that veiled the man's face was familiar. But the assassin couldn't place where he'd heard it before.

For a few seconds, there was only silence.

The man's smoldering eyes glinted in the dim light. There was an uneasy calm as he regained control of himself, and then he spoke crisply. "We have jets to ambush the American helicopters; they will be destroyed before they ever reach Bhaliq. And your success is guaranteed even if the Americans should somehow survive. Just do as you have been told."

Qaim bowed, his pointed grey beard touching his chest. "I will do as you wish."

"And see that no one outside your family knows about this."

"Upon my word as the *shayka* of my family," Qaim promised, knowing his reputation as the progeny of four generations of ruthless assassins would undoubtedly carry great weight with his client.

Qaim bowed again, then retired from the room, his eyes darting in all directions.

Outside, the Arab shivered in the cool night air and held his breath as he stole toward the little-used side entrance leading to the narrow street. He opened the door and peered into the darkness, fingering the meticulously-oiled Czech CZ-83 hidden under his robe. The dark street was empty, barely lit by moonlight.

Qaim squeezed through the narrow doorway, retrieving an iron key from his robe and twisting it in the hasp of the door he closed behind himself. Then he dropped the key into the hidden pocket of his robe.

As he stole catlike through the darkness, his ears detected the scrape of a sandaled foot against the packed earth of the street. Silently whirling around, he gripped his pistol and peered into the shadows.

There was no one on the unlit street but a blind

talib, sleeping in a doorway. The sightless man suddenly reached out and grabbed at Qaim's robe. Qaim jerked away in disgust and shoved his pistol back into its hiding place.

Qaim pushed past the beggar, who extended his chipped cup hopefully and croaked, "Alms for an old sightless—"

"Quiet, you fool! Not tonight."

Ten minutes later, Qaim unlatched the wooden door leading to a darkened courtyard. In the distance a goat bleated.

Four baked-mud brick houses faced the courtyard. Three were homes to Qaim's sons, their wives, and children. The fourth two-room structure was Qaim's own household; inside, his two wives and four remaining children slept, unaware of his nocturnal adventure. His slippered feet shuffled across the dusty courtyard, making him painfully aware of the shabbiness of the surroundings.

He unconsciously hid in the deep shadows of the acacia tree that blotted out the half moon hanging in the sky above the courtyard. The stars twinkled like diamonds, forever beyond his reach.

If he and his sons succeeded, Qaim realized, things would change; it would mean wealth—great riches unlike anything his family had ever known, even in its heyday as hirelings for the *amir* of the Tuaregs. His family might even be able to resettle in Bhaliq.

And if we fail? Qaim wondered.

He pulled his black burnoose tighter around himself, and forced the idea from his mind. Qaim would see to it that they would not fail.

A breeze whistled down the shadowy street, raising a cloud of dust. It jiggled the wooden gate that stood between the courtyard and the narrow avenue, then rattled the dry leaves of the acacia overhead.

Qaim shut his eyes for a moment to the airborne grit and inhaled deeply. He knew he must do what had to be done. There was no time to waste. There were plans to be finalized if he was to be prepared by tomorrow night. He melted into the blackness at the front of the nearest flat-roofed house.

Tomorrow the Americans would arrive. And even if the jets failed to stop them, the men of Qaim's household would be prepared.

C H A P T E R

1

The briefing took place in the division commander's conference room. The paneled chamber was located on the second floor of a three-story brick building on the grounds of Fort Bragg, North Carolina, at the northern edge of Fayetteville. The old fort served as home base for airborne combat units of the U.S. Army, including the anti-terrorist Delta Force team.

Around the oak table sat six Night Stalkers pilots and the Delta Force Team leader. Division Commander Captain Louis Warner stood at the head of the table, studying the faces of the soldiers in front of him.

Warner was a veteran of Vietnam, where he had flown Huey helicopters on combat missions. He was a skilled pilot and justly deserved the respect accorded him by the Night Stalkers and others in Task Force 160, which he led.

Rake-thin and balding, he spoke to those gathered in the room with a trace of a Brooklyn accent. "Operation Desert Wind is *not* going to be a milk run. Up front, I want to remind you that 'assassination' is an Arab word. Many of the governments that deal with East Sahra, where the mission will be conducted, consider assassinations to be a *normal* political weapon. You may have to deal with anything from a bomb run to a dagger hidden in the clothing of someone next to you."

He paused to retrieve a paper match from its book, then lit the cigarette that had been hanging unlit in his mouth. He continued. "Adding to the complications, East Sahra doesn't have an airstrip big enough for us to land our transports. Morocco, which is north of East Sahra, has given us permission to land one—and *only* one—transport. So if you run into trouble in East Sahra, you're literally going to be on your own. We *might* be able to land a jet or drop in some paratroopers. But it would be days before they'd get to you."

The division commander punched a button on the AViiON workstation keyboard in front of him. A map appeared on the monitors nestled in the surface of the table in front of each soldier at the table.

"As you can see," Warner said, "the country you're headed for is aptly named. 'Sahra' means desert; East Sahra is located in the Sahara Desert within this small area intersected by Morocco and Western Sahara north of Mauritania." The commander traced the region on his viewscreen with a light-pen so it was highlighted on each of the other monitors.

"The climate will be tough on your choppers. It's hot—even though it's winter there—and dusty. Annual rainfall is two inches—in wet years." Warner paused to tap the ash from his cigarette into a stained metal tray.

"The country was established by Morocco's

King Hassan in 1985, in part to reward the Bedouin tribes who helped Morocco in its bloody fight in Western Sahara against the Polisario Front."

"Wasn't the Polisario Front supported by Libyan military aid?" Captain Jefferson Davis Carson asked with a southern drawl. Known as "Oz" to the pilots around him, the tall, lean pilot from Virginia would be the air mission commander in charge of actually executing Operation Desert Wind.

"That's correct," Warner nodded. "Libyan and Algerian aid. That alone makes your mission dangerous. The conflict ended when Libya and Morocco signed the treaty that created the Organization of African Unity. The treaty was dissolved in 1986, but by then Morocco had established its hold on the region, and East Sahra had become a sovereign country on its own." Warner drew a deep breath through the cigarette, then exhaled smoke.

"The blood feuds between the tribes involved on either side of the war go way back, too. The Sa'adi and Banu Hilal tribes that form a third of the population of East Sahra were loosed on the Berbers in A.D. 1052 by the Fatimid caliph; they reduced Libya from a garden to its present desolation. We're looking at centuries of hatred just waiting to break out."

Warner typed briefly on the keyboard again and punched the enter key. The faces of two men appeared on the monitors. "The guy on the right is King Abdul Karim Khadduri, the ruler of East Sahra. The clean-shaven fellow on the left is his son, Sulaiman. Don't make the mistake of thinking these folks are camel jocks; Sulaiman has a bachelor's from

Harvard. The king is a regular in Paris and has brought in hi-tech solutions for many of the problems facing his country. While they aren't embracing the West, they *are* exploiting its brains and technology. The king's set up one of the best educational systems in Africa."

"What type of government are we looking at?" asked Sergeant Hoover, one of the Night Stalkers pilots.

"The government itself is a Constitutional monarchy modeled after Morocco's, with the King having broad powers," Warner answered. "The king is a Tuareg—one of the most influential of the four Bedouin tribes. I might add that the Tuareg is the only tribe among the Bedouins that's matrilineal; keep that in mind so you don't commit a faux pas.

"The current problem facing the government is that the king has pretty much excluded the other three Bedouin tribes, the Sa'adi, Qahidi, and the Banu Hilal from having any say in the government. So a civil war's been simmering there almost from the time the country became independent. Over the last year, that situation has heated up.

"Fortunately for the government, gold was discovered in the Jebel Ahvaz mountain range along the northeast border. It's enabled King Khadduri to purchase a fleet of V-22 Osprey gunships, improve the food production of the country, and modernize his capital city, Bhaliq. The king is interested in stabilizing his country and has agreed to negotiate with the other three tribes to cease the hostilities. And that's where we come in."

Warner carefully ground his cigarette into the

ashtray, then looked up. "The king has requested that the U.S. government transport his son to the first round of negotiations and guarantee his safety there. Since the State Department sees East Sahra as a potentially big player in the future and wants to help get things sorted out there, the president has agreed to the king's request. So your job will be to take the prince into a neutral—and as yet undisclosed—meeting place within flying distance of Bhaliq *and* keep him safe once you get him there. It's not going to be an easy assignment."

Warner studied the faces around the table. "All right, let's get to the details."

King Abdul Karim Khadduri waved aside his bodyguard and eased himself into the back seat of the armored Cadillac limousine. The king settled his stocky frame into the cushioned seat and adjusted his turban. Without thinking, he smoothed his gray, bushy eyebrows and drooping moustache. Then he looked up and smiled at his son as the young man got into the car from the opposite side. The limousine's air conditioning felt like an oasis in the desert, cool and refreshing.

"I can't believe how soft we've become," the king remarked, half to himself. "I used to wander with my father all across the desert in the blazing sunlight. Even in the summer. Now I can hardly stand to be outside even in the coolest part of the year. Air-conditioned cars. I wonder what my father would think of us."

"We aren't soft," the prince countered. "We have adapted to the new ways necessary for our people to survive. Maybe you're just getting old and set in your ways," he gently teased the older man. Unlike his father, the prince was clean-shaven and wore a three-piece suit rather than the traditional *djellaba.*

The king smiled and slapped his son lightly on the cheek. "My troublemaker. I see much of your grandfather in you."

"The Japanese seemed anxious to build the weapons factory here," the prince remarked, changing the subject.

King Khadduri glanced out the window at the busy street. "They were too anxious," he said quietly. "We will wait a week and let them fidget. We need the factory, but gold mines or not, our country has only a limited amount of money," he sighed.

The king eyed the hot sun that bore down on the black car. "Take us back to the palace," he ordered the driver after the burly bodyguard had got into the front. The locks on the doors snapped and the driver put the car into gear.

The limousine sped down the wide road leading directly to the palace. Branching off the thoroughfare were narrow streets bustling with activity. Delivery trucks and bikes, shoppers, and tradesmen jostled each other as they went about their business.

The prince unlatched the lilliputian bar built into the car, smiling to himself as he always did when he opened the refrigerated unit. Only Americans would put a bar into a car being customized for Moslems, he thought. Did they not know Moslems were commanded by the Koran not to drink alcoholic beverages? Americans were such an odd combination of arrogance, ignorance, and friendliness, he mused.

And now they thought they were coming to help his country make peace with itself. He retrieved a bottle of orange juice from among the cans of soft drinks that filled the bar.

"Want something?" Sulaiman asked his father.

The king shook his head. "I hope we succeed with our plans for the peace conference."

"There's nothing to worry about, father. And this may be the only chance we have to create a country of our own. The risks are worth taking to establish a nation for our people. When we go ahead with—"

"What's that up ahead?" the king interrupted as the driver honked the horn.

The prince looked out the front of the windshield. Waves of heat rose from the concrete street and made the palace in the distance shimmer. About thirty feet ahead, a camel driver struggled to get his kneeling beast out of the roadway. Blocking the other half of the avenue was a truck that had apparently swerved to miss the animal, tipping over and spilling its cargo of apples.

"Turn around," the bodyguard ordered. "It may be a trap!"

"Nonsense," the prince said. "Our guards can help get this mess cleared away. We are in no rush."

The bodyguard spoke into the handheld radio he carried and the soldiers in the jeep behind the king's limousine got out and jogged forward to help the man get his camel out of the way. A crowd gathered as the men worked to clear the street.

A moment later, a bomb in the Volkswagen parked on the avenue exploded.

CHAPTER

2

Eighteen hours after Commander Warner's briefing, Operation Desert Wind went into effect. It called for the deployment of six Night Stalkers helicopters along with a Delta Force Team platoon. Four of the choppers were MH-60K special operations aircraft; the other two were McDonnell Douglas AH-64 Apaches.

The helicopters' crews flew the choppers from the Simmons Army Airfield just west of Smith Lake at Fort Bragg, to Pope Air Force Base four-and-a-half miles northwest. At Pope, the six helicopters were partially disassembled and prepared for transport in a C-5A Galaxy. The helicopters, their ground and air crews, and the Delta Force troops, dressed in desert-tan "pebbled-camo" battle-dress uniforms, were soon aboard the transport, headed for north-western Africa.

The C-5A was like a building with wings. Its cargo hold was longer than the Wright Brothers' first flight; the plane itself was almost sixty-eight meters wide and over seventy-five meters long. Just the paint on the aircraft weighed nearly a ton. From its camouflaged wings hung four powerful TF39-GE-1C turbo-jet engines.

The MH-60Ks and AH-64s were stored on the lower deck of the transport, carefully strapped in place so they couldn't shift during the flight. The Night Stalkers personnel, Delta Force troops, and an Air Force security team rode in the pressurized and air-conditioned upper deck of the C-5A.

As they flew at 25,000 feet over the Atlantic, most of the men catnapped, the droning roar of the engines covering the voices of the few men who conversed softly.

The C-5A shuddered in air turbulence. Oz glanced at his crew chief, SP4 Mike Luger, who sat nervously on one of the web-seats across from him. Luger had the body of a jogger and was a bundle of nervous energy. Although he never got airsick on choppers, he occasionally became ill in the enclosed transports when the ride got bumpy.

"I hope Luger brought his barf bag," Oz whispered to O.T., who sat next to him.

"I made sure he did," O.T. smiled grimly. Harvey Litwin was the warrant officer for Oz's MH-60K. He doubled as the door gunner and crew chief. Like Oz, he had actually seen action during the closing days of Vietnam. Because of his age, he had become known as "old timer"—O.T. for short. He often referred to the others in his aircrew as "the youngsters" and was appalled by their lack of knowledge of recent historic events.

The plane seemed to stumble in the air and Luger rolled his eyes upward and bent forward in his chair. O.T. smiled at Oz and shook his head.

Oz leaned back and closed his eyes again, allowing his mind to wander. He wondered if he'd remembered to make his car payment. He recalled with relief that he'd remembered to put the cat out the night before but he had to ponder the question of the car payment for a moment. Yes, he was almost sure he had.

Then the pilot swore under his breath. Here he was worrying about a two-hundred-some-odd dollar car payment when he was traveling half way around the world to fly a killing machine worth millions of dollars. And ferry around a prince worth what, billions?

And he was worried about some damn car payment and a yellow tomcat!

It's one freaking weird life you lead, Oz told himself. I wonder what my father would have thought of this kind of life? he mused. The army was a lot different when Jake Carson fought in the Philippines at the tail end of World War Two and then in Korea.

Jake Carson was the sole survivor of a platoon that had been overrun by North Koreans. He'd become completely disillusioned with the war after that and had concentrated solely on surviving until he was finally transferred home. He had capitalized on his GI bill to go to college, graduating with a double-major in chemistry and teaching.

Jake had worked his way to the top of the chemistry department at Norfolk State University in Bridgewater, Virginia. The closest he'd ever come to battle again was evading the political infighting at the college and plinking at tin cans in the back yard with his son, firing an old .22 Colt Woodsman.

Professor Carson spoke little of his wartime experiences. Only after Oz had served in Vietnam did he understand his father's reticence about discussing WWII and the "Korean Conflict," as the media insisted on calling it.

Oz had discovered that those who had never seen combat couldn't understand what it was like and most who had didn't want to be reminded.

Professor Carson had been bitterly opposed to his son's decision to join the army. Oz had started college at the University of Virginia but had been disillusioned by the anti-war tone of many at the school. He decided to drop out and enlist.

He'd announced his plans during supper one evening in May.

"That's the damndest idea I've ever heard!" his father exploded.

"Jake," his wife Leone interrupted. The professor silenced her with a cold stare.

"You fought for freedom," Oz contended. "Now it's my turn."

"Fought for freedom! Look at what's going on over there. You won't be fighting for freedom. Vietnam's got a dictatorship that's just as bad as any communist government ever thought about being."

"But if we don't stop the communists there, they'll take over that entire part of the world," Oz objected.

"Spare me the high school civics class rhetoric," his father erupted. "Hell, the average U.S. citizen didn't even know where Vietnam *was* before this war. You think it'd make a bit of difference if one backward little country full of slant-eyes went communist? Hell, most of the Vietnamese don't think enough of their country to fight for it." He slapped a helping of mashed potatoes onto his plate and passed the bowl to Oz's brother Mike.

"Damn it," Jake Carson continued, "you'd be fighting for a corrupt government and a bunch of people who don't care whether the communists take their country or not. Is that what you want to sacrifice your life for?"

"Once the communists get a foothold there, the other countries will follow," Oz countered.

"Oh, yes, the domino effect," his father snickered as he sliced into his steak. "A fine theory to sucker starry-eyed fools into the service. Face the facts, Jeff. China's already communist. That hasn't affected Japan and never will. You think Australia's going communist if Vietnam falls? No way! The only countries that are going to follow suit are the other little backwaters that aren't worth spit."

He pointed his knife toward his son. "Besides, I've seen how the military operates. They don't just waste supplies and equipment. They waste men. A good leader is taught *never* to get close to his men so he won't hesitate to sacrifice them during a manuever!"

"Well, my mind's made up," Oz said softly.

Jake Carson snorted. "Don't confuse me with the facts, huh. My mind is made up, is that it? If you enlist in the army, Jeff, then you're a goddamned fool!"

Oz stormed from the room. He left by bus the next morning.

Despite his disillusionment with the way the U.S. Army conducted the war, Oz threw himself into the conflict. He often took chances that terrified his buddies, appearing all the while to be impervious to fear. He had become convinced that America was right about fighting in Vietnam.

As the last of the American troops were pulled out of Vietnam, Oz had remained in the army and eventually was asked to join the elite Night Stalkers force responsible for ferrying CIA agents and anti-terrorist squads worldwide.

Oz was jolted out of his reverie when his transport hit another pocket of air turbulence. He looked across the aisle and noticed Luger was once again using his air sickness bag.

The trans-Atlantic flight of the C-5A ended at the short airstrip at Tan-Tan in southern Morocco.

"I don't know what to think about East Sahra," O.T. remarked conversationally, as he stood beside the others. They waited for the C-5A's hydraulic system to lower the massive rear ramp of the cargo plane. "Anyplace that doesn't have an airstrip long enough to land a fair-sized jet has to be a little backward."

"The king of East Sahra isn't interested in having tourists come to visit," Oz explained to his warrant officer as he squinted into the bright sunlight that came streaming through the opening door. "And not having a runway also guarantees that you won't have Soviet-made carriers loaded with Libyan troops dropping in, either."

O.T. chuckled. *"Both* of those are good reasons not to have a long airstrip, so I stand corrected."

An oppressive wave of heat pressed its way into the carrier as the front and rear hatches of the plane locked open. An air force lieutenant behind them was completing his orders to the security platoon.

"Keep sharp," the lieutenant finished. "We can't afford any incidents. Now get a move on."

The air force troops ran past Oz and O.T. and tramped down the cargo hatch ramp. The soldiers wore desert battle-dress uniforms, combat boots, and blue berets. They were fully armed with M16A2 rifles, M203 grenade launchers, and M60 machine guns.

After getting the all-clear sign from the security team, the helicopter crews sauntered into the hot sunshine. The air felt dry and tasted of dust. Oz slipped on his mirrored Gargoyles sunglasses and unzipped his olive-green flight jacket. He felt the sweat exude from his body.

"You know," O.T. said, rubbing a beefy hand over his shaved head, "I had the misfortune of spending my honeymoon in Key West, Florida, during August. The heat was unbearable, the insects fierce, and my new bride and I argued most of the time. I've never been so miserable in my life outside of actual combat. Except for the lack of humidity, I'd say this place has all the allure of Key West in August!"

Oz nodded grimly. It was going to be a long week even if things didn't get dangerous.

*　　*　　*

Designed for air transport, each of the four MH-60K helicopters had rotors and tail fins that could be folded into a compact load, a hydraulic cart to reduce the pressure in its landing gear, and a towing assembly and steering bar that enabled the choppers to be easily pulled and guided through the cargo hatches of the transport.

The six-man army crews in charge of assembling each helicopter were supervised by the air force load-master as the choppers were lowered down the cargo ramps using the C-5A's winch. Once clear of the transport, the choppers were rolled off the dusty tarmac for assembly.

Oz's MH-60K was put together by a sweaty team directed by Sergeant Bruce Marvin, a neckless bulldog of a man with a hairy barrel chest. Sergeant Marvin glanced at the sun and scowled, then growled at one of the five men he supervised, "You know the drill, Sucro. Git with it."

The team first labored to raise the chopper's engines and increase the pressure in the landing gear with the hydraulic cart temporarily placed inside the front of the passenger compartment. These operations gave the aircraft its normal, taller profile.

The color-coded rotors were unfastened from their blade support poles and retainers on the right and left sides of the fuselage near the tail. Four team members then used the blade handling pole to unfurl the blades. Two men held the ringed bottom of the pole to position it; those holding the cables extending from the top of the pole did the actual work in swiveling the blades into position. Each blade was rotated forward to allow the support link and bracket to be removed, then rotated back.

"Watch your fingers," Sergeant Marvin shouted to Private Sucro, who was standing atop the helicopter.

Sucro, waiting to lock the blades in place, jerked his hand out of the way and grinned sheepishly at the sergeant.

Marvin shook his head. The private whose job it was to secure the blades into their flight position seemed determined to get his hand smashed between the blade and the main rotor sleeve.

Within forty minutes of being wheeled out of the transport, the four MH-60Ks and two AH-64 Apaches were nearly ready for flight. The ground crews checked the loading manifests and carefully replaced the components that had been removed from the helicopters before they had been packed into the C-5A. When that job was completed, each team leader reported to his army air crew.

By ten o'clock, Moroccan time, the sun had baked the airstrip and turned the desert into an oven. An oppressively hot wind whipped fine grit over the landing gear of the helicopters, marring the paint with tiny scratches. The American flight crews climbed into the helicopters, groaning as they encountered the even hotter air trapped inside the cabins.

Both the MH-60Ks and AH-64s were armed since there were several countries that would profit if the tribes in East Sahra became engulfed in a civil war. While the chance of an actual attack on the

American air convoy seemed remote, the Night Stalkers were nonetheless prepared as were the Delta Force troops who accompanied them.

Each of the MH-60Ks carried four weapons pods on modified external tank suite struts. The pods were arranged in what had become the standard armament for such missions. On the right side of the rack was a pod containing double 7.62mm machine guns and a twelve-tube 2.75-inch rocket launcher pod. To the left of each helicopter was a 532 countermeasure dispenser to defeat heat-seeking missiles and a sister pod containing a pair of TOW missiles. Door gunners on either side of each MH-60K manned 6-barreled, 7.62mm Miniguns.

The two AH-64 Apaches each sported an M230 30mm Chain gun mounted to the underside of the chopper. The gun was slaved to the FLIR, or forward-looking infrared viewer coupled to the gunner's helmet as part of the IHADSS, or integrated helmet and display sight system. This system used infrared sensors and an on-board computer to enable the gunner to engage targets day or night. On each of the AH-64's pylons hung a quartet of weapons pods consisting of twenty-four 2.75-inch ballistic rockets and eight Hellfire missiles that could be guided to their targets with a laser target acquisition and designation sight.

After the pre-flight checks were finished, Oz switched on the helicopter's intercom. "O.T., Luger, how are things back there?" he asked the two gunners sitting in the compartment behind him.

"Sergeant Marvin's team is buckled into their seats," O.T. answered matter-of-factly. The ground crew rode in the helicopter so they would be available to service the machines and make minor repairs. The other three MH-60Ks each carried a squad of heavily-armed Delta troops.

Oz received clearance from the air traffic controller, then switched his radio to its ABN frequency and ordered all the choppers into the air.

The engines of all six helicopters started, their rotors increasing in speed with a low-pitched, furious thumping that raised a storm of desert sand around the machines, causing a "white out" as the pilots lost their ability to see what was around them. Using the helicopters' multi-mode radar and FLIR, the pilots lifted the choppers from the manmade sandstorm, carefully watching their scopes to maintain their spacing and avoid a collision.

To the small crowd of civilians that had collected outside the chain-link fence surrounding the crude airfield, the American choppers seemed to materialize out of the sandstorm. The black machines lifted above the field and gracefully assumed their positions, the MH-60Ks forming a diamond pattern flanked by the two AH-64 Apache gunships. As the Moroccans watched, the machines darted away from the airstrip like a formation of giant dragonflies.

They flew over the shantytown of tents, tin sheds, and mud-brick homes that had grown haphazardly along the outskirts of Tan-Tan. When they were beyond the town, the chopper pilots switched to their terrain following/terrain avoidance radar. The TF/TA enabled them to stay below radar surveillance and reduced their chances of being detected. The helicopters remained in tight formation, skimming the rolling hills of rock and sand as they headed toward Bhaliq.

Oz spoke into the small intercom mike fastened to his helmet, "Death Song, let's talk to Desert Hen."

"I'll have the COMSAT in a second," Oz's co-pilot/navigator replied as he sent the code toward the military communications satellite hanging high above Africa. Rail-thin with dark skin and jet-black hair, the Native American navigator operated the computer keyboard with a relaxed, self-confident grace.

Oz glanced through the chin window at the miles of sun-bleached sand below, broken only by an occasional green clump of welwitschia struggling just to stay alive. The pilot next checked the vertical situation display which listed all aspects of the flight path, horizon, and heading of the MH-60K, along with its radar altitude and the pitch of the chopper's blades. He knew he couldn't afford to get the slightest bit off course in the desert.

"The satellite is interrogating our computer," Death Song said. "OK. We're locked in. You can go ahead."

Oz triggered the radio switch on the control column in his right hand. "Desert One calling Desert Hen. Over."

"This is Desert Hen," Captain Warner's voice came back, climbing in pitch to sound somewhat like Donald Duck as the hot desert air distorted the radio wave. "Go ahead, Desert One."

"We're heading toward our objective. No sign of trouble. Over."

"Keep your eyes open and apprise me of your situation when you reach your objective."

"That's a roger, Desert Hen."

"And be sure to stay right on course. Our sponsors have been very emphatic that you stick to your course so they won't mistake you for intruders."

"Will do."

"That's all I've got for you now," Warner said. "Good luck, Desert One. Over and out."

Oz switched his radio back to ABN frequency, "Desert Two through Six, this is Desert One. We'll continue our course as planned and keep a sharp lookout for bandits. Anybody got any problems? Over."

Oz waited a few seconds. There was no answer. "All right then," he said. "Use your radios only if you've got an emergency or spot unfriendlies." Oz then gave the "Silence, silence, silence" command, informing the helicopter crews flying with him that they were to maintain radio silence until they reached Bhaliq.

Twenty kilometers southeast of the Night Stalkers' position, three French-made Mirage jets skimmed along the desert floor. The armed planes were devoid of identification; they flew on a flight path that would intersect that of the American convoy.

C H A P T E R

3

A moment before the Volkswagen exploded, a blue pickup truck with a load of plate-glass windows came rolling to a stop alongside the king's limousine. The force of the detonation was diverted and dampened by the truck. The blast ripped through the pickup, shattering the glass into fragments that splattered against the Cadillac like hail. Though shaken, the king and prince, as well as the driver and bodyguard in the front seat of the limousine, were protected by the steel plate and Kevlar armor of their vehicle.

Others on the street were not so fortunate. Almost everyone within forty feet of the Volkswagen was killed instantly by the concussion and fragments of metal and glass that slashed through the air. Windows in the front of the buildings on either side of the explosion were shattered, their jagged shards whipping through offices and businesses to gash and slice those inside.

"What in heaven's name!" King Khadduri exclaimed, his ears still ringing from the explosion. A trickle of blood ran down his temple. "These poor

people, we must help them," he murmured as he
pulled at the handle beside him to open the car door.

"No, your excellency!" the bodyguard bawled.
"There may well be a second bomb. Please give me
your permission to get you away from here at once."

The king looked through the spalled glass at the
bloody bodies lying in the street.

"He's right, father," Prince Sulaiman whispered urgently. "We must leave at once. Call the
hospital and get ambulances sent immediately," he
ordered the guard. Then he leaned forward and
spoke to the driver. "Get us to the palace by another
route as quickly as possible."

The bodyguard eyed the crowd, watching for
any sign of further danger.

The black MH-60K and AH-64 helicopters
sped across the hot desert. The rolling dunes below
Oz's craft looked like a frozen sea of sand, broken
by rocky cliffs that formed islands of eroded earth
in the silicon ocean.

The aircraft's shadow danced above the uneven
surface below like a ghostly doppelganger. In the
distance ahead of the chopper, Bhaliq, the capital
city of East Sahra, twinkled in the mirage as the afternoon sunlight seared the pink sand.

Oz tried to ignore the sweat that was collecting
inside his olive-green helmet and at the back of his
Nomex suit. The sunvisor of his helmet was lowered
over his eyes to filter the bright sunlight that poured
through the windscreen of the chopper.

"Desert One, Desert Three. We've got—"

Static cut off the transmission. There was a flash

behind and to Oz's left, followed by the thunderclap of an exploding rocket. Oz turned in his seat to glance out the port to his left.

Desert Three tumbled through the air, its tail rotor ripped apart by the fireball of a missile. The pilot of the MH-60K fought to ease the helicopter to the ground as the machine rotated ever faster around its remaining main rotor. The chopper arched downward and crashed into the barren sand, raising a storm of dust.

Oz instinctively triggered his radio. "Break!" he ordered the remaining choppers around him. Over the intercom he instructed his crew: "Arm our weapons. Death Song, give me the rockets and machine gun. Get the TOW ready."

The Mirage F1 jet that had felled Desert Three roared past the remaining five American helicopters, its machine guns chattering as the Night Stalkers scattered before it. Two of the jet's missiles flashed beyond the dispersing choppers and exploded harmlessly on the ground, creating plumes of dust and rock.

Oz pulled on the collective pitch lever, taking his helicopter upward so fast it pinned everyone to their seats with the added G-force.

Death Song watched for other incoming jets on his radar screen. He spotted a blip, barely discernable as it flashed over the ground clutter. "We've got another bandit—no two—coming in low directly behind us!" he warned Oz.

A volley of rifle fire rattled off the side and window next to Oz. "Where's that coming from?" Oz demanded.

"Friendly fire," O.T. yelled on the intercom. "Desert Four's dogs are firing out the side doors."

"Desert Four," Oz called, "tell your Delta troops to cease fire. They're hitting us with their strays!"

"That's a roger," the pilot of Desert Four called back. His voice was distorted as the electronic jamming from the incoming jets threatened to completely disrupt the radio message. "The LT's already chewing the Delta newbie's ass," the pilot relayed.

As the first Mirage rolled in the distance ahead of the helicopter formation, Oz continued to lift his chopper into the air. He kicked his left pedal so the helicopter would face the incoming jets, keeping the control column forward to maintain speed. His sharp turn threw everyone in the chopper to the right, their seatbelts restraining them during the violent maneuver.

The radio hissed and whistled with static. Then Oz could discern a garbled message from Desert Five, one of the AH-64 Apache pilots. "We've got the first one covered," the pilot announced.

A fire-and-forget Hellfire missile on the AH-64 blossomed to life on its pylon. The seven-inch diameter rocket quickly accelerated to Mach 1.17 as it chased after the distant jet that had been targeted by the nose laser controlled by the gunner in the chopper. The Cassegrain telescope in the nose of the Hellfire locked its microprocessor logic circuit onto the image of the jet.

The jet slowed to bank and readied for another attack run, unaware of the oncoming missile tailing it. The electronic circuits in the Hellfire automatically activated the four canard controls to home toward its target. Within the blink of an eye, the Hellfire caught the jet, its warhead detonating with the impact. Secondary explosions of the plane's missiles and fuel tank split the plane apart as it tumbled toward the earth.

The second Mirage was now nearing the scattering helicopters. The jet came in low, the machine guns on its wings blazing as it passed the MH-60K to Oz's right, strafing the chopper with bullets.

O.T.'s Minigun whined in a long explosive string of shots from the gunner's window as Oz swung the helicopter into position to fire his 2.75-inch rockets at the now-retreating plane. He hit the red button on the control column under his little finger.

One of the rockets in the pod to the Oz's right hissed from its tube and chased after the plane, missing it by a wide margin as the jet pilot veered and managed to avoid the unguided projectile.

"Desert Four, look out, he's on your tail!" Desert Three warned over the radio as the jet swooped like a hawk at the low-flying helicopter skimming the desert's surface.

There was a burst of jamming that blotted out the reply, then another message broke through: "I've got the second bandit," the Apache pilot in Desert Six yelled into the chaos that was erupting on the radio.

"Third jet's coming in," Death Song warned Oz.

Oz squinted at the area where he knew the plane must be approaching as he tried to locate the jet visually. A moment later, he saw the flash and smoke as the Mirage launched a Faucon II missile toward the helicopters ahead of it.

"Missile!" Oz warned his crew and passengers as he fired one of his rockets and then threw the chopper into a steep bank.

The MH-60K helicopter Oz piloted dropped toward the desert floor. He flew so close to a low cliff of rock and sand that it seemed as if the walls that came speeding toward the chopper were only inches away. The noise of the chopper's rotors boomed from the rock face and echoed down the narrow valley.

"It's locking onto us!" Death Song warned as the distinctive sound of the Mirage's continuous wave fighter radar illuminated them to the semi-active radar homing guidance system on the Faucon II missile. Death Song quickly released a flare and chaff from the countermeasures pod, hoping one or both would confuse the oncoming rocket.

As Oz jockeyed the helicopter along the cliff walls, the aerial inside the nose radome of the missile continued to sense the helicopter and altered the hydraulic controls in its delta wings to home onto its target. The guidance system of the advancing rocket ignored the flare Death Song had released as it sputtered on its tiny parachute. Then the Faucon II lost its target as it neared the scattered reflections of the foil chaff.

The missile turned, chasing an electronic shadow as it passed through the cloud. Then it suddenly re-acquired its target, but not fast enough; it smashed into the cliff face before it could gain on the fleeing MH-60K.

The approaching Mirage fired another Faucon II as Oz rose from the arroyo in the desert floor. The missile acquired the MH-60K to Oz's right and started homing in on it.

"It's got you, Desert Two!" Oz warned. "Bank left!"

The pilot of Desert Two, Sergeant Rick Hoover, muttered through clenched teeth as he received Oz's warning, his reply lost in the heavy static of the radios. The Faucon II homing in on him continued in a long arc, gaining speed as Hoover banked his helicopter in an effort to avoid the missile.

The pilot dropped his chopper, creating a sandstorm as he hurtled over a high, crescent-shaped *barchan* dune and then dropped behind it. The missile lost the MH-60K for a moment, then regained it as the jet that had released it darted over the helicopter.

Oz watched as the co-pilot in Desert Two released a cloud of chaff that tumbled in the wake of the chopper's blades. The Faucon II missile was nearly on top of the MH-60K when it hit the chaff. The rocket lost Desert Two at the last moment and rushed past the chopper, missing the arc of the helicopter's rotors by only meters. But the nearness of the chopper activated the proximity fuse in the projectile's logic circuits.

The warhead exploded with a blast that rocked the peaceful valley with its thunderclap. A fraction of a second later, flak rattled against the skin of the chopper, penetrated the main rotor assembly, and tore into the air intake scoop. The chopper's engines made a grinding sound and the blades shook ominously.

"Mayday, Mayday," Hoover called as his chopper lost the little altitude he had. "We're going down." Oz watched for only a moment as Desert Two splashed into the sand.

"If I get us lined up, can you take that third bastard?" Oz asked Death Song.

"I'm ready," the navigator answered evenly.

The pilot kicked the right rudder pedal on the floor in front of him so the helicopter faced the fleeing Mirage.

"Take him," Oz ordered, then triggered his radio, "We've got the third bandit. Who's got the second?"

"We do. Desert Five does," the voice of one of the crew in the AH-64 Apaches called. "We've blocked him from—. No wait. He's—"

The radio message ended abruptly. Another blast ripped through the valley. The fiery wreckage of Desert Five whirled out of control and slammed into the face of a cliff.

Oz swore under his breath and concentrated on keeping his chopper aligned with the second jet that Death Song was targeting.

The co-pilot/gunner next to Oz grasped the TOW missile's joystick controls as he monitored his target on the pull-out virtual image display. The VID high-resolution "TV" sight was linked to the chin-mounted FLIR on the helicopter. The plane came into line on the screen.

Death Song initiated the launch.

The TOW rocket was boosted from its launch

tube on the left of the MH-60K. A fraction of a second later, the TOW's rocket engine ignited with a puff of smoke and the missile's eight fins popped into place in a blur of motion. The TOW quickly accelerated to its maximum speed of slightly over one thousand kilometers per hour.

The voice of Desert Six crackled over the radio. "We've got another pair of jets coming in low from the east."

Oz glanced from his side door and saw the telltale smoke trail that marked another rocket launch. It was far away, but still a concern to the pilot, who knew that air combat was often over before the victim even got a chance to see what was firing at him. The exhaust stream showed that the rocket was headed for one of the other choppers. Oz triggered his radio, "Desert Six, looks like that one's headed your way."

"I see it," Desert Six answered. The pilot took his helicopter into a steep dive, dropping behind a hill of sand out of Oz's sight.

Death Song continued to guide his TOW toward the Mirage that was now trying to elude it. The American carefully watched the display screen, altering the missile's course with the joysticks; the rocket responded instantly as it received the electrical control commands over the twin wires unspooling from it.

As the TOW overtook the Mirage, the jet's pilot rolled in an effort to elude the on-coming missile.

But Death Song had anticipated such a frantic maneuver. The TOW struck before the pilot could dodge. Nearly three kilograms of high explosives detonated in the engine of the fleeing Mirage. The plane tumbled out of control as the pilot ejected. Fire and metal rained onto the desert below him as the wind caught his parachute.

"We've got a jet coming in on our tail," Luger warned Oz over the intercom.

A clattering of machine gun bullets from the Mirage ripped along the side of the MH-60K. Then the jet pulled up and raced past, rocking the chopper in its wake.

Oz tapped the fire button on the control column with his little finger. Three rockets jetted from their pod and chased after the fleeing airplane. A moment later, one of the rockets smashed into its wing tip and exploded.

The plane wasn't severely damaged, but it was sufficiently impaired to remove it from the fray if the pilot didn't want to risk being an easy target. The Mirage shook slightly as the pilot fought it around and headed into the desert to get out of the range of the helicopters.

"Missile at three o'clock!" Death Song warned.

Oz shoved forward on the control column, increasing the pitch of the rotor's four blades for maximum speed. Simultaneously, he dropped the collective pitch lever, forcing the MH-60K into another steep descent that rendered the occupants weightless as they dropped.

Death Song's fingers danced on the counter-measures buttons. The chaff dispenser showered metal flakes into the air behind the chopper. The cloud of confetti scattered the radar beam guiding the missile toward the American chopper.

"Hard right!" Death Song warned as he watched the oncoming missile on the radar screen.

As the navigator released another cloud of chaff, Oz threw the control column to the right, kicking the right pedal at his feet in the same instant. The MH-60K turned. Oz shoved the control column forward and lifted the collective pitch lever to stop their descent just a few feet above the sand as they skimmed along the desert floor.

The rocket hissed past. But it came close enough to cause the sensors in its warhead to trigger the proximity fuse. The warhead detonated.

Fragments of the missile peppered the exterior of the MH-60K. A hole appeared as if by magic in the plexiglass windscreen beside Oz. The aircraft shook in the pressure wave of the explosion.

"I've got it," Desert Six called. The Apache AH-64 circled above Oz's chopper and released a Hellfire. The missile targeted the Mirage.

A moment later, the jet was torn apart as the warhead struck its fuel tank. The jet completely disintegrated in the massive fireball that erupted.

A second explosion rocked the hot air a moment later. Oz turned in his chair to see the final Mirage plunge into a sand dune.

"This is Desert Four," the pilot called, his voice quivering from the adrenalin in his bloodstream. "We got the last one!"

"Four, check Desert Two for survivors. Do you see where they crashed?" Oz radioed, aware that all radio interference had disappeared with the downing of the last Mirage.

"That's a roger. Four heading down."

"Desert Six," Oz called.

"Roger, Desert One, this is Desert Six."

"You circle and provide cover while I search for survivors in the wreckage of Three and Five."

"Will do."

"We've got more company," Death Song warned over the intercom. "I've got six—no eight—blips coming from the south."

"Desert Four and Six, stay in the air," Oz ordered. "We've got eight more bandits coming our way."

CHAPTER

4

Oz watched as the eight aircraft approached the American helicopters.

"They're coming in too slow for jets," Death Song said as he watched the radar scope.

"VTOL or prop, maybe?" Oz mused. He toggled on his radio. "Let's sit tight until we see what we're facing," he ordered the two other airborne choppers. "Desert Two and Three," he radioed the damaged aircraft that were on the ground, "have your dogs get out and into the hills. Then you abandon your choppers. If worst comes to worst, you ought to be able to reach Bhaliq on foot in a couple of days' time."

"Should we destroy the choppers?" Desert Three queried from the ground.

"No, not yet," Oz responded. "But stick close to your birds for a while. If we get creamed, go ahead and destroy them. Over."

"We're evacuating the choppers now," radioed Desert Two's pilot. "Lieutenant Victor asked me to inform you that his men may be able to take some of the bandits with the Dragon rockets they're packing. Over."

"That's a good idea, Desert Two," Oz replied. "But tell them to hold their fire until the enemy starts shooting. We don't know for sure that these aren't friendlies. Over."

"Will do."

"All my passengers are out and headed for the hills," Desert Three called. "We'll be signing off now."

"Our dogs are all off, too. Desert Two signing over and out."

"They're in range for our Hellfires," the pilot of Desert Six, the remaining AH-64, radioed.

"Hold your fire, Six," Oz ordered. "They're approaching in an awfully tight formation for an attack. I'm beginning to wonder if—"

"Desert One," interrupted a heavily-accented voice, "this is ES-7 of the East Sahra military forces. We're approaching you from the south in eight Osprey. Over."

"We have you on our scopes, ES-7," Oz called back. "We're glad to hear you're friendlies. We have three of our choppers down and will be needing medical assistance. Over."

"We followed the battle on our radar and came as quickly as we could get into the air. Our apologies for not getting here sooner."

Oz paced along the hot desert sand as Sergeant Marvin assessed the damage to the two MH-60Ks. Six of the East Sahra V-22 Osprey aircraft flew overhead to give air cover to the Americans on the ground. The tilt-rotor V-22s were armed with nose-mounted 12.7mm Miniguns and air-to-air missiles. Four of the V-22s traveled like conventional airplanes with their twin blades tilted forward; but two had taken positions to the north and east of the crash sites where they hovered like helicopters with their twin rotors swiveled upward.

Sergeant Marvin squinted in the bright desert sunlight. "I think we can get Desert Two back into the air using parts cannibalized from three since only the tail and landing gear of Three were damaged when the missile downed it."

"How long will it take?" Oz asked.

Marvin pulled at his ear lobe and thought a moment. "The East Sahrans don't have any way to transfer the chopper into Bhaliq by air. But one of their pilots thought a small winch and hoist could be transferred out here. Basically we'll have to work here in the desert with just the tools we're carrying. So it's going to take at least eight, maybe ten hours at best."

"It would be good if we could have that chopper by this evening when we ferry Sulaiman to the conference," Oz said. "So try to do it in four if you can. It could probably meet us at the conference site tomorrow," he added, "but I hate to have it traveling alone."

"I'll push it, but I'm not making any promises," Marvin answered.

"In the meantime, get your crew to transfer the armament from Three to the other choppers. I'd like to take them into Bhaliq with full armament."

"No problem," Marvin said. "We can do that in about twenty minutes."

Moments later, Oz contacted Warner via radio link through the COMSAT hookup. The man-made moon that was in geosynchronous orbit over the desert relayed the pilot's voice around the world and Warner was quickly apprised of what had happened.

"Captain Carson," Commander Warner instructed, "it's essential that you continue to Bhaliq. Ferry two of the Delta squads into the capital. You should be able to complete the mission with the three remaining choppers."

"Sergeant Marvin believes he can get one of the downed MH-60Ks back into the air in under eight hours," Oz responded. "I hate to split our forces for that long, but I'd like to have the extra chopper. Shall we try to repair it? Over."

"Yes," Warner answered. "You'll have to leave one of the Delta squads behind with Sergeant Marvin and his crew anyway. Have the troops destroy what's left of Desert Five and Two after Marvin's taken what he needs in the way of parts. The East Sahrans have volunteered to transport the dead and injured to Morocco. We'll have them transported back to the states from there. Over."

"Sir," Oz began hesitantly, "the injured Delta troops have requested permission to continue the mission. Their wounds are only minor—nothing the medics can't handle. And they'd like a chance to even the score if we're attacked again. Over."

"I'll leave that decision to you."

"I'd like to keep them, sir."

"All right then. Keep me informed of any developments. Over."

"Will do, Desert Hen. Over and out."

5

Four of the tilt-rotor Osprey V-22s escorted the three Night Stalkers helicopters over the capital city of Bhaliq while the remaining four stayed with Marvin and the wrecked choppers.

Oz followed the lead V-22 toward Bhaliq. The pilot gazed from his side window and studied the small city sprawled across the desert.

The Jebel Ahvaz mountain range extended into the dark blue of the horizon to the northeast. At the outskirts of the community were plastic-domed greenhouses that covered several acres of the desert and looked like glass bubbles floating over the sand. Solar collectors glistened in the sunlight, filling the spaces between the domes; the electrical generators powered the air pumps which kept the plastic spheres pressurized. The solar collectors also provided the energy for air conditioners to cool the domed farms to optimum temperatures for the rows of trees and tiers of vegetables. The crops themselves needed only one-tenth the area and one-twentieth the water of those of conventional open-field farms.

A deep-pump water station, conspicuous with

its concrete and steel solidarity, stood among the plastic domes. The complex drew fossil ground water from deep under the desert and pumped it to the domed farms. Since the water contained too much alkali and salt for normal agriculture, the crops in the greenhouses were salt-tolerant varieties developed in Israel, the U.S., and Saudi Arabia. A reverse-osmosis filtration plant next to the pumping station generated fresh water for the citizens of the city.

As the air convoy passed over the town, the shadows of the American choppers and V-22 Ospreys darted over the tiny, sunbleached, mud huts below. Even at its outskirts, the city had been carefully laid out in square grids and lacked the haphazard appearance of many older cities in Northern Africa.

The smaller homes soon gave way to residences of four and five rooms, many with spacious courtyards. At the center of Bhaliq, the architecture became a study in contrasts as the old collided with the new. Large homes of rock and sun-dried brick were interspersed with huge geodesic domes housing industrial complexes, schools, and parks. A few of the businesses displayed tall towers that jutted fifty to sixty feet into the air, catching the winds high above the city and funneling the cool air into the structures below.

A long, wide thoroughfare lined with three-story, Western-style buildings of glass and concrete cut through the very heart of Bhaliq. At the exact center of the boulevard stood King Abdul Karim Khadduri's palace which embraced a courtyard that stretched around six acres of luxuriant grounds. As they passed over the complex, Oz noticed an anti-aircraft battery and air-to-ground missiles nestled into fortified positions in the roof.

The V-22 Ospreys escorting the Americans rotated their blades upward, slowed, and hovered over the marble landing pad at one end of the palatial courtyard.

"Desert One," the the pilot of lead Osprey radioed to Oz, "you now have permission to land at this position."

"Thanks, ES-7," Oz replied. "We appreciate your help."

"It is our honor," answered the East Sahran. "We pray that your mission will help bring peace to our country. Over and out."

Oz circled the landing pad, studying the huge flag hanging over the palace in order to judge the wind speed and direction. The pale blue banner was embellished with a white crescent and a ring of white stars; it blew toward the south in the dry desert wind.

"This is Desert One," Oz called to the two American choppers following him. "We'll go in first. Six will land to our left, Four, to our right. Four, have the Delta troops stay inside your chopper until we find out what the score is. Over and out."

The pilot lowered the collective pitch lever and countered the wind with the control column. The chopper dropped toward the landing pad, flanked by the Apache and the other MH-60K.

Oz climbed out of his chopper and observed an army officer and another man approaching him from one of the tree-lined lanes that wound through the courtyard. The civilian was a rail-thin man. As he approached, the few wisps of hair he possessed were swept back toward his balding crown by the wash of the rotors. He ducked his head as he neared Oz, unsure of the rotor clearance above him.

"You must be Captain Carson," the man said, stopping in front of Oz and extending a scrawny hand. "I'm Bill Cookingham, U.S. Ambassador to East Sahra. I'll be serving as your guide and interpreter during the next few days."

"Nice to meet you, sir," Oz responded.

"And this," Ambassador Cookingham motioned to the tall military officer beside him, "is General Ali Kader Mahala, head of the East Sahra armed forces."

"General Mahala," Oz said, forcing himself not to salute when the man extended his hand.

The general smiled, showing his even, white teeth. He stood ramrod straight in his tan uniform, the distinctive crescent and star insignia of East Sahra emblazoned on his right shoulder.

"Your men put up quite a fight," General Mahala told Oz. "I'm surprised you were able to counter jets so well."

"We finally prevailed," Oz answered, "but we lost some good men and at least two of our helicopters in the process."

Oz noticed Lieutenant Victor approaching from the other MH-60K and introduced him as the leader of the Delta Force attachment. The lieutenant stepped forward and shook hands with the ambassador and general.

"I've sent our best ground crew and a portable

crane to the crash site," General Mahala informed the three Americans. "Perhaps they will be of help. I know working on machinery in the desert can be an almost impossible task."

"Thank you, sir," Oz said.

"Yes, it is much appreciated," Ambassador Cookingham added. Then the ambassador turned to Oz. "Captain Carson, General Mahala's military aide will take your men to a rest area while the East Sahran Military mechanics refuel your helicopters. The fuel trucks will be along shortly. In the meantime, the palace guard," Cookingham nodded toward a group of troops marching toward the landing pad, "will be protecting your choppers until you leave with the prince this afternoon."

Oz hesitated a moment, then ordered Lieutenant Victor and his men to accompany the air crews to the rest area.

As the four men prepared to part, Oz turned once more toward the East Sahran military leader. "Thank you again for your help, sir," he said, shaking the general's hand.

Captain Carson and Ambassador Cookingham strolled along the marble walkway that wound through the verdant garden. They met a detachment of East Sahran soldiers marching toward the choppers. The troops lifted their rifles and machine guns smartly as the two Americans passed. Oz appreciated the amount of drilling the troops must have undergone to execute such a flourish.

Each of the twenty soldiers was clad in a tan uniform emblazoned with blue braid. The headgear was the traditionally-styled blue *keffiyeh* which afforded the troops protection against sand, sun, and winds. Most of the men carried SAR 80 rifles with 30-round magazines; every fifth soldier held an Ultimax 100 squad automatic weapon with a short assault barrel and a 100-round drum magazine.

Cookingham turned to speak to Oz as the two men sauntered toward the white palace ahead of them, glistening in the sun. "Don't worry about your choppers, Captain Carson. General Mahala participated in some of the most savage fighting between the Moroccans and the Polisario Front; you can bet that no one's going to be getting near those helicopters. As for the palace grounds, they're quite secure."

Oz nodded. "I noticed the missile complex to the north and the rocket and artillery battery on the palace itself as we came in," he said. "I don't think much is going to get in here unless there's a full-scale attack on the city."

Cookingham smiled and then was silent for a moment before speaking. "We don't have much time, I'm afraid. I've been in touch with Commander Warner. And, by the way, I want you to know, I'm sorry you ran into so much trouble on the way in to Bhaliq. I'd thought this was going to be a simple mission for you guys; obviously I was wrong. Anyway, the State Department is wondering if you have any guesses as to the identity of the jets that attacked you? They're out for blood in Washington, but they don't have any leads."

"They were French-made Mirage jets but they were unmarked. They came in low from the east, but they might easily have come from any direction and vectored from that bearing for the attack."

Cookingham nodded. "I've been told that the East Sahra soldiers in one of the planes circling your wrecked choppers radioed in a few minutes ago. They found the pilot that had ejected from one of the jets you shot down, but he died of internal injuries shortly after they picked him up. He appeared to be an Arab but had to ID papers on him. So I guess that's a dead end for now."

The ambassador stopped speaking as they passed a gardener pruning a flowering magnolia. In the distance, a peacock cried plaintively. The two Americans rounded a bend in the walkway and suddenly found themselves confronted by the huge marble and concrete palace that towered at the end of the path.

The building looked like something from the *Arabian Nights*. Its lacy arabesque carvings and tiled patterns intertwined with the flowing lines and columns of the facade. Upon closer inspection, Oz noted that the highly adorned building had been constructed in such a way as to make it an impregnable fortress, despite its heavy embellishment. Here and there, he could just barely discern the black barrels of .50-caliber weapons nearly hidden in weapon ports within the shadows of the ornamentation.

"I think I should tell you now," Cookingham said quietly, "that things are even more tense than your briefings may have suggested among the four Bedouin tribes. I don't know what's going on. And of course the King's been keeping us at a distance since the car bomb attack—"

"Car bomb?"

"Yes, just this morning. Seventy-eight people were killed and at least three hundred injured." They resumed their walk along the towering front facade of the palace. "The biggest hotel and the front of a shopping mall were nearly destroyed. Fortunately, the king and his son escaped with only minor injuries. There've been rumors on the street the last few days that outsiders were going to try to derail the peace conference, but the king hadn't put much store in all the talk. The attack you experienced, however, would seem to bolster the rumors. Here's the palace entrance," he said, gesturing.

Oz cautiously stepped through the arched entryway supported by twisting, Byzantine columns. He was surprised to note that the guards within were armed only with narrow-bladed scimitars. As one of the sentries hauled open the florid gold-inlay gate for the two Americans, however, Oz noticed the gun slits and TV surveillance cameras behind the guards. Very slick, the pilot thought to himself.

The entrance hall of the palace felt icy cold to the Americans, after the baking sun. Oz's boots echoed on the marble flooring as he and the ambassador quickly made their way down the long, gloomy hallway.

"Despite the attack," Cookingham continued, "the prince insists that the peace conference should go ahead as scheduled. I don't really think I need to brief you on what to expect tonight at the reception for the prince being given by the four Bedouin tribes. It will be pretty much of a feast—with all the excellent Bedouin dishes.

"This way," the ambassador continued as he guided Oz down another corridor. "Commander Warner asked me to inform you that we still can't get one of our eyes-in-the-sky into position over the meeting site. They should have gotten one before the mission," he added, "but it's impossible now since they're being used to verify whether or not the Soviets are conforming to our new treaty."

"It would have been a big help if we could have gotten some coverage," Oz admitted. "But if I can position one of the choppers on a hill, we should be able to maintain a watch without using much fuel or manpower. And if my ground crew can repair one of the MH-60Ks, we'll be in even better shape tomorrow."

As the two Americans turned down a narrow hallway adorned with tiled floral patterns stretching from the floor to the high arched ceiling, Oz glanced back over his shoulder.

He saw an East Sahran soldier stealing around the corner that the pilot and the ambassador had just rounded. The man paused and then turned back in the same direction he'd come when he saw the American studying him.

Oz wondered why the soldier was trying to overhear the ambassador's briefing.

6

At 1700, Oz lifted his MH-60K from the sun-baked airpad in the palace courtyard. The hot afternoon air blew through the open side doors of the chopper, offering little respite to Prince Sulaiman, Ambassador Cookingham, and the Delta Force troops who rode inside.

"Keep a sharp lookout," Oz warned the pilots of the AH-64 and MH-60K accompanying him. He wheeled his chopper in the air and checked his VID to be sure they were on the correct course heading. Once the helicopter was aligned on its route, he shoved the control column forward, quickly bringing the aircraft to its maximum speed of 290 kilometers per hour.

In the city below them, traffic choked the narrow streets as workers made their way home. Cars, trucks, donkeys, and camels traveled alongside each other; people dressed in traditional robes jostled men and women in Western-style clothing. Many people on the streets, aware of the mission, waved at the choppers hurtling overhead.

The conference site was in the middle of nowhere, forty kilometers southwest of Bhaliq near Quarkziz, an ancient village built around a small oasis. Not holding the meeting in a city made perfect sense to the Bedouins, who had been nomadic until the 1950s. Only then were efforts made to settle the desert dwellers in Arab cities, since modern transportation and an increasing population curtailed the need for century-old trade routes. Also in keeping with the ways of the nomads was the fact that the conference room was to be a large tent that was now slung under the helicopter Oz flew.

The catch, the American pilot realized as he shot over the city, was whether the rendezvous point had been kept a secret. By the time the king and the other three tribal leaders had reached an agreement, a lot of people knew the "secret" location.

Oz knew this to be a concern of Prince Sulaiman as well, whom he had met briefly before they boarded the American chopper.

When Ambassador Cookingham introduced the two men, Oz bowed slightly, as the ambassador had coached him to do. The American soldier had been told that he should show respect for the prince, but that he should take care not to appear subservient; the ambassador was concerned that Americans be perceived as citizens of a sovereign foreign state outside the jurisdiction of East Sahra.

"Commander Carson," Prince Sulaiman said in perfect English, a slight grin on his dark face as he met the pilot's gaze. "I believe your men call you Oz. I have to wonder how you acquired that name, captain, since it comes from an American story or movie, if I recall correctly."

"Yes," Oz said, slightly abashed. "Frankly, it's a little embarrassing, sir. When I first started flying 'copters, my captain remarked that I must think I was some sort of wizard to attempt the stunts I pulled. My buddies started calling me the Wizard of Oz—somebody who appears to be someone special but who's really a fake. After a while, the nickname was shortened to Oz and it stuck."

"Well," the prince grinned, "from what I've heard about the dogfight with the Mirage jets, you've lived up to your reputation. When we asked your secretary of state for the best combat helicopter pilot in the United States, he produced your name without a moment's hesitation. I think you're more wizard than fake these days, captain."

Oz felt a slight blush creeping up his neck. "Well, sir, I hope you don't change your mind once we get into the air."

The prince laughed. "I hope not, too," he said. "Now let's get on board your magic carpet. I only hope *I* can work as much wizardry on the ground when we get there as you've worked in the air today."

Now the American convoy was clearing the southeast corner of Bhaliq. The three choppers exchanged positions in the trail formation, with the Apache AH-64 helicopter taking the lead, Oz going to second position, and the remaining MH-60K, which had a large fuel bladder slung under it, at the tail. Oz hoped this would confuse anyone who might have observed the prince leaving the city in the lead aircraft.

The three choppers remained in tight formation

skimming the rolling sand dunes as the pilots switched to terrain following/terrain avoidance radar to evade surveillance. As Oz activated the auto control, he remembered the morning attack.

The Americans had been on TF/TA before when they were ambushed, which meant that whoever had attacked must have known their route and their approximate time of departure—although that could have been supplied by someone near the air strip at Tan-Tan. If an informant in the East Sahra government had leaked the information, then the location of the conference had probably been divulged as well.

"Desert One, this is Desert Three, come in please," a voice over the radio interrupted.

The pilot toggled the radio switch on the control column with his first finger. "This is Desert One, go ahead, Three."

"Our repairs have been completed, captain, and we've been refueled with a portable fuel bladder. We'll be ready to follow you in twenty minutes. Over."

"That's great, Three. Hold on and we'll relay the coordinates to you. Over."

Oz coupled Death Song's helmet mike into the radio link so the co-pilot could relay the position of the peace conference to Desert Three.

The 1750A/J73 dual-mission computer in all the army choppers had been encoded at the start of the mission with a data cartridge. This contained the navigation way-points in southern Morocco and East Sahra, as well as communications frequencies, data about possible targets, and current codes for the U.S.

military's IFF (interrogate friend or foe) more commonly known as "Squawk." By updating this database from the cockpit's terminal keyboard with the information Death Song relayed to him, the navigator in Desert Three could locate the site of the peace conference without allowing anyone intercepting the message to locate it as well.

After Death Song finished sending the coordinates, Oz took over the radio. "You get all that, Desert Three?"

"That's a roger. If our computer isn't screwed up, we'll be catching you by late tonight."

"Let's hold off on that, Three. I have a feeling things are going to be jumpy enough tonight without having a chopper coming in after dark. Why don't you move to a new position to avoid detection and then hunker down overnight and come in tomorrow morning."

"Will do, Desert One. But remember us tonight while you're feasting and watching the belly dancers. Over."

"We'll definitely remember you," Oz answered. "Enjoy your MREs. Over and out."

The pilot switched off the radio and scanned the barren horizon. Then he spoke into the intercom. "Still clear, Death Song?"

"Scope's clear and I'm not getting any nearby radio traffic," the co-pilot answered.

"Let's hope it stays that way," Oz murmured.

An hour later, the Night Stalkers were over the conference site. The evening sky was cloudless, the air calm. Oz glanced through the side window at the array of sun-bleached tents which the Bedouins who arrived first had pitched in the sand. Most of the dwellings were traditional *badawi* tents constructed of woven black goat's hair supported by poles, although a few were of canvas.

The camp was located inside the two horns of a *barchan* dune that towered above the campsite. Nearby was an arroyo, a dry stream bed that only became a body of water during rare desert rainstorms.

Oz noted the rifles carried by almost every Bedouin on the ground. Both Ambassador Cookingham and the prince had insisted that the strong moral code of the Bedouins, which required giving protection to guests, made the chance of anyone harming the prince or Americans very remote. The throng below appeared friendly enough, waving at the helicopters, but Oz hoped security wasn't going to be a problem. He thought about the fight that could erupt even with the ancient weapons the tribesmen carried.

"Desert Six," Oz called over the radio. "Satellite around the camp until we position the tent and fuel bladder and get our passengers snuggled in."

"That's a roger, One."

"Four, stay in position until we get settled."

"Roger."

"O.T.," Oz said over the intercom, "I'm going to lower us almost to the ground. Guide me in and release the tent when it's time. Things look pretty wild down there, so keep a sharp lookout. We're going to have to be careful not to squash any of the conference members."

"Will do," O.T. answered. "I've got the floor panel open. Take us in."

As the helicopter inched downward, Oz was relieved to see the Bedouins gave the chopper a healthy clearance. A cloud of dust and fine sand was whipped into the evening air as they neared the ground.

"Another foot," O.T. said.

Oz carefully eased the collective pitch lever down.

"That's good," the warrant officer shouted. He unlatched the cable holding the tent and the huge bundle of striped canvas dropped onto the sand. "All right, you can take her up," O.T. directed.

"Is the scope still clear?" Oz asked Death Song when they were back in the air.

"Nothing on the radar but Desert Six and Four."

Oz triggered his radio. "Six, we'll use the east end of the camp for our landing pad. Desert Four, you go in and put the fuel bladder down next to the dune, and let Lieutenant Victor get his troops out to escort the prince. Then land on the dune overlooking the camp. We'll use that position to watch the area with radar after dark. After you're parked on the dune, we'll come in second. Six, keep an eye on the scope and come in after we get the prince into one of the tents."

Oz waited for the MH-60K carrying the Delta Forces squad to drop its fuel and land, staying clear of the dust cloud the machine kicked up as it neared the desert's surface. Within five minutes, the troops had been deployed, the aircraft was atop the dune, and its blades wound to a stop.

Another cloud of dust erupted as Oz brought his chopper into position, lowering it toward the sand below. Because the ground was obscured by the "white out," Oz eased the chopper to the earth as slowly as possible.

As the MH-60K bumped the ground and the pilot cut the engine, one of the Bedouin tribesmen standing in the midst of the crowd of well-wishers, squinted into the storm the flying machine had raised and fingered the dagger hidden in his robes.

C H A P T E R

Oz had hoped to get Prince Sulaiman into one of the tents after landing.

But that was not to be.

When the tribesmen saw the prince as he leaped from the chopper, a cheer rose, and a celebration that sounded more like a war than a party exploded. The Bedouins fired their weapons into the air and danced around their leader, laughing and shouting.

"Captain," Lieutenant Victor yelled, "how the hell are we going to protect him in all this? This is like a damned riot!"

"Do your best," Oz yelled back. Given their taboo against harming a guest, the prince was more apt to be trampled than assassinated for now, the pilot thought to himself. "Have your men stay on the perimeter to watch for intruders. We'll just have to trust the tribesmen to protect him from any real harm because I don't see any way we can stop this."

Oz walked to the front of his helicopter, opened the pilot's door, and climbed in. He grabbed the control column and toggled on the radio. "Desert Six, this is Desert One. Come in please."

"This is Six. What the hell's going on?" the pilot of Desert Six asked. "We took several hits from small arms when we crossed above the camp. Over."

"Some of the crowd are firing their guns into the air to celebrate," Oz answered. "We can't see you from the ground now that the sun's set, and it's too noisy to hear you. Did you suffer any damage?"

"Just to our nerves. No apparent harm to the chopper. Over."

"Is the radar picture still clear?"

"Still clear."

"In that case, come down ASAP and join the party."

"We're coming in. Over and out."

After the impromptu welcome for Prince Sulaiman, the Arab tribesmen worked furiously to get the conference tent unfolded, spread, and erected. The men toiled in the beams from the landing lights of the helicopters. Their shadows were thrown on the distant *barchan* dune facing the camp.

The Arabs worked quickly and efficiently, despite the fact that many of them had never participated in erecting so large a structure. As far as Oz could tell, no one was really in charge of the operation, but everyone seemed to know his job. Once the tent was erected, the men and a few veiled women who had appeared from the smaller tents scurried in and out from the various shelters to the meeting tent carrying hair rugs, tables and pillows.

Within an hour's time, the conference tent was furnished, and Oz and the other American Army personnel who were not on duty guarding the camp were seated on cushions around clusters of small tables. The dim light of the oil lamps cast a yellowish glow over the faces gathered there.

Some of the Arab men were attired in loose-fitting *djellaba* robes with long sleeves and hoods. Others wore the similar but heavier burnoose. A few, including Prince Sulaiman, were garbed in shirt-like jackets with a belt tied around the waist and baggy pants. On their heads were either turbans or the traditional *keffiyeh*. Their footwear was light, resembling boots or slippers.

The women who stood waiting to serve the food for the banquet wore beautiful caftan robes and embroidered baggy trousers reserved for such special social functions. Gold bracelets and rings adorned their arms and fingers. All the women wore veils, their dark eyes twinkling in the lamplight as they watched their leader.

Prince Sulaiman rose and the crowded tent grew silent.

He cleared his throat and spoke a few words in Arabic, then turned to Ambassador Cookingham and the American soldiers seated around him, "We welcome you, our American friends," he began. "Although we Bedouins are not a mighty nation like the United States, we, too, value freedom above all else. We have reason to be proud of our independence. Before Mohammed walked the earth, we *badawi* had learned to live by our own moral code, a code that emphasizes courage, generosity, and loyalty. Tonight you are our guests. We thank you for coming to help us as we forge a nation of our own."

He bowed toward the Americans and resumed his place at the low table.

Ambassador Cookingham arose to respond.

He spoke each sentence first in Arabic, then in English. "On behalf of the United States," he said, "we thank you for this banquet tonight. It is our pleasure to attend your meeting. We know that you will succeed in creating a new nation, and we are happy to be a part of your efforts. It is an honor and a privilege to be here during this historic event."

Cookingham resumed his place next to Oz and the room became quiet. "It's your turn to speak," the ambassador whispered to the pilot.

Oz stood up, silently cursing the ambassador for not informing him earlier that he would be expected to say a few words.

The pilot licked his lips and began. "We are honored to be here and are glad to be in a position to offer what little help we can during your conference." As Oz spoke, Ambassador Cookingham translated his words into *al-lugha al-wusta,* the "the middle language" that could be understood by most Arabs regardless of their local dialect.

"I have noticed that all of you carry firearms and knives; some of you even wear swords," Oz continued. "We American soldiers, like you, carry arms to preserve our freedom and the liberty of our friends. But arms cannot answer all problems or make men live together in harmony. It's therefore my hope that your conference will be successful and that you will be able to achieve the goal of becoming one nation of free Bedouin people."

There was quiet. Then those around the tables cheered as Oz sat back down.

"Very good," Prince Sulaiman whispered, clapping Oz on the back. "I think you would have done as well in politics as you have in the military," he laughed, then he turned back to the men sitting at the low tables around the room. "Now, let us eat!"

There was a murmur of agreement.

Within moments, steaming trays of food were carried into the room by the veiled women who were wives of some of the men in attendance. There were bowls of rice, and soups made from beans, lentils, and onions; side plates of squash, dates, olives, and almonds; oranges and clusters of grapes; and pastries made with honey and almonds.

Hot mint tea, a traditional drink for guests, was placed before each of the men sitting at the tables. After the entrée plates had been set at each place, the main dish was produced. This, Cookingham explained to Oz in a whisper, was the traditional couscous, which consisted of steamed wheat served with vegetables, lamb, and a soup-like sauce.

As the final trays of food were being brought into the tent, Oz's attention was drawn to the man who approached the table at which Prince Sulaiman sat.

The pilot lost track of what the prince and the ambassador were saying and concentrated his full attention on the approaching figure. Oz was certain he had seen the flash of a naked steel blade in the light from the oil lamps.

Majid Qaim and his three sons penetrated the sprawling tool shed where they had been told the jeep was hidden. The vehicle was there with its trailer hitched behind, loaded with spare gas cans, food, and enough water for their mission. Qaim examined one long, narrow roll of canvas at the side of the trailer containing the Mauser rifles promised him.

Two things went wrong shortly thereafter. First, the vehicle wouldn't start. Then Qaim's youngest son, Parim, who was guarding the door, alerted them that someone was coming.

Qaim debated whether they should try to get the Mauser rifles out of the canvas but decided there wouldn't be time to do that and load the rifles as well. He motioned for his sons to hide in the back and all four swiftly crossed through the shadowy building.

Within seconds, a pot-bellied watchman with long, muscled arms rattled the door to test its lock. Finding the entrance open, he cautiously entered.

"Who is in here?" he asked in *al-lugha al-wusta*

to ensure he would be understood by any Arab who might be hiding in the building. "I know you came in, I saw you." The beam of his flashlight darted around the room, resting for an instant on the jeep and then stabbing at a pile of old tires along the wall.

The guard whirled around as something clattered to the floor at the back of the tool shed. The beam of his flashlight bathed a large jerboa scurrying along the tool bench, its rat-like feet causing a screwdriver to clank across the counter surface and fall to the floor.

Perhaps I was mistaken, the watchman thought as he continued to search the building. In fact, it was probably unnecessary for him to even bother; the owner had specifically told him to leave at dusk, but he had decided to work his regular shift. After all, he had told himself, a good job is hard to come by. Putting in extra time to protect his employer's possessions would make his job more secure. And if he succeeded in capturing an intruder, so much the better. The village of Quarkziz, where he lived, prided itself on its low rate of crime; he would be hailed as a hero.

Better check the back room next, he decided; there was no one in the front.

The watchman crept toward the doorway, his boots scraping against the sandy concrete. He extended his flashlight ahead of him like a saber and drew his Colt .38 revolver from its worn leather holster as he entered the back room.

Studying the shadows in the corner of the room, he saw the movement on either side of him too late. He was suddenly grabbed, both arms pinioned from behind, his flashlight and revolver wrenched from his hands. The ensnared watchman struggled futilely to break free. Then there was a sharp pain in the small of his back, followed by a flow of warm, sticky liquid.

He cried out as another slash fell across his throat and his captors dropped him to the floor. The flashlight shining in his eyes seemed dim, and his ears started to ring. Within moments he was unconscious; five minutes later, he was dead.

Parim continued to shine the watchman's flashlight into the man's face; the sightless eyes stared back at the four men clustered around the body and the light reflected off the dark pool it lay in.

Abruptly Parim cried out, gagging at the sight.

"Get back to the jeep, all of you," Qaim barked, remembering how, as a boy, he had felt sick the first time he had witnessed a murder. "Go! Now!"

Parim stood hesitantly.

"Go stand guard again," his father ordered the boy.

The youngest son looked questioningly into his father's eyes, then walked slowly across the concrete floor to the doorway.

Qaim knelt and wiped the blood from his dagger onto the watchman's shirt. We might as well be Shi'ites instead of Sunni Muslims, he thought. First they were going to become known as kidnappers, and now they had been forced to kill outside of their contract.

The assassin returned to the jeep.

"The battery cable is loose," Kamel announced from under the hood of the vehicle. He carefully tightened it, using a wrench from the nearby table while Qaim cut the ropes securing the rifles to the trailer.

Kamel slammed the hood down and climbed into the jeep.

The vehicle refused to start.

Kamel tried the starter again and the engine coughed to life.

"Quickly," Qaim told his sons as they piled in. The father ran to the large garage door and lifted it so they could back the jeep out. Within minutes, they were chugging along the narrow streets darkened by dusk.

Qaim placed a rifle between the two front seats and glanced at the nighttime sky, checking the time by the position of the first few evening stars. We are going to be late, he thought. If he had believed in prayer, he would have prayed they wouldn't be too late.

CHAPTER

9

The day of laboring under the blistering desert sun was the worst Sergeant Marvin could ever remember. The hot drifting wind and alkali odor of the heated sand seemed to have completely destroyed his sense of smell.

The heat had taken an even greater toll on some of the others. Sucro had dropped from heat stroke within the first two hours, shortly after they'd transferred the ordnance from Desert Three to the other helicopters. Then Lieutenant Carlos Rivera and Captain Pete Ullrich had dropped in their tracks within minutes of each other, also victims of heat stroke.

That left Sergeant Marvin the highest ranking member of the detachment of soldiers with Desert Three. It also gave him responsibilities he didn't relish. But despite the extra work and the worry of keeping everyone from succumbing to the heat, Marvin had succeeded in getting Desert Three repaired using spare parts cannibalized from the wreckage of Desert Two.

When darkness finally unscrolled across the desert, Marvin was exhausted. He shivered in the cooling night air. "Don't wake me unless it's an emergency," he instructed Specialist Rogers, the Night Stalkers co-pilot who had drawn the first watch to monitor the radio during the night.

Marvin found a clear space among the sleeping soldiers and huddled into a poncho. He fell asleep immediately, too exhausted to worry about scorpions or anything else.

The jeep's headlights stabbed the darkness. It appeared to Qaim that they were finally making up for lost time as they wove their way along the floor of the arroyo. Only once did they have to detour when their path was blocked by an *erg* dune, which had apparently invaded since the stream bed had last cut through the valley.

Then their good fortune came to an end.

"By the Prophet's eyes and ears," Majid Qaim swore under his breath as the left rear tire of the jeep rattled in its wheel well. "Stop!" he commanded.

Qaim jumped from the jeep before it had completely halted and stumbled in the gravel. The heat from the rough surface of the earth rose through the soles of his shoes. He shined the watchman's flashlight on the tire and saw it was obviously flat, just as he had known it would be.

"We will have to remove the trailer from the hitch to get to the spare," Talam told his father.

"Hurry," Qaim demanded. "Parim, hold this light so we can see what we're doing."

The sweaty men labored to change the tire. Twenty minutes later, the jeep was ready to go again.

"We'll be lucky to get to the camp by midnight," Qaim raged, pulling his *keffiyeh* across his mouth and nose to keep the fine grit that was blowing from getting into his lungs. And it looked like the wind was blowing up a sandstorm! Qaim realized, that if that occurred before they reached the prince . . . !

It was almost possible for Qaim to believe that Allah was doing his best to make their mission a failure.

"Hurry," the father urged Kamel as the younger man got behind the steering wheel.

Inside the MH-60K resting atop the *barchan* dune overlooking the camp, Specialist Robert Newman continued to study the radar scope. The green phosphorescence of the screen reflected off his black skin and made his brown eyes shine. Satisfied there was nothing of concern in the air around the camp, he wiped the scope-screen of the dust that had blown in, leaned back in his seat, and stretched his tired muscles.

Newman's face seemed to wear a perpetual grin, which had gotten him into trouble more than once at boot camp, and which might have been responsible for his missing the party below him tonight. As one of the newest co-pilots on the mission, he'd been assigned the first watch on the scope. He didn't really mind missing the banquet all that much; exotic food didn't agree with him anyway.

Suddenly he heard the rattle of metal and stared through the open side door of his chopper, squinting into the darkness; but the young black could see nothing. He glanced at the luminous dial of his Glycine military watch, and noted it wasn't time for his replacement. When the rattling occurred again, the young co-pilot was certain someone was on the dune with him.

He snatched his night vision goggles from the seat to his left, removed the protective caps over the front lenses, and lifted the device to his face, switching the unit on at the same time.

The view screens over his eyes sputtered to life, giving him a bright, monochrome picture in green and white of the camp below him. Newman searched the face of the dune but saw no one. He shifted his head, searching frantically.

Still nothing.

There! Painted in green and white by the NVG, two figures slowly advanced up the small draw in the sand, fifty yards away, their clothing flapping in the wind. One carried a rifle slung over his back; the other didn't appear to be armed.

No, wait, Newman thought. The second figure carried a big pack under one arm, a bag that, upon closer inspection, looked suspiciously like a satchel charge to the army co-pilot.

He reached toward the radio, then realized he didn't have time to contact the captain, sitting far below him in the tent. By the time he'd explained what was happening, the two figures would have reached the chopper. He'd have to act immediately on his own.

The co-pilot unsnapped the cover on his holster and drew his Beretta 92-FS, continuing to hold the NVG in his left hand as he leaped from the open door of the chopper. His booted feet sank several inches into the free-flowing sand.

Holding the NVG awkwardly between his knees, he cycled a round into his pistol.

He knew he had to hurry. He couldn't afford to allow the intruders to get close to the MH-60K.

Everything seemed to be happening in slow motion.

Oz half-stood as Saddam al-Bakr approached Prince Sulaiman's table. The pilot was only vaguely aware of Cookingham's voice as the ambassador asked if something was wrong.

The American pilot reached for his Ruger pistol, his eyes riveted on the approaching man's hands. al-Bakr drew the long-bladed dagger from his robes. As the P-85 cleared its holster, Oz realized he wouldn't have time to jack a round into his pistol; instead, he'd have to utilize his firearm as a club.

With his free hand, the pilot shoved the prince to the side. Prince Sulaiman sprawled over, kicking the table in front of him so dishes of food slid in a noisy cascade off its edge. The glistening blade in al-Bakr's hand missed the prince by inches, slashing the air where he had been.

Oz slapped downward with his gun hand, the pistol striking against the blade of the knife but missing the knife-holder's wrist, which had been the pilot's target.

al-Bakr lifted his blade with surprising speed, its mirrored surface slashing through the air toward Oz.

The pilot jerked back, but not quickly enough. The blade sliced into his forehead above his right eye, instantly creating a spurting stream of blood. Bedouins and Americans alike bellowed in outrage, and chaos erupted in the tent creating a babble in English and Arabic as they rose to aid Oz.

The flickering oil lamps were reflected from the razor-sharp dagger as al-Bakr sliced at the nearest Bedouin who rose to his feet and lunged at him. Oz exploited the distraction by leaping onto the low table in front of him and vaulting toward the knife-man.

al-Bakr perceived the flash of movement and whirled on the oncoming American pilot, his knife gliding through the empty air as he pivoted.

Oz's booted foot smashed into al-Bakr's fore-arm, diverting the upward jab that would have been a fatal, disemboweling cut had it followed through. The pilot's body collided with al-Bakr, knocking him off balance. Oz grasped the forearm of the hand holding the knife and swung his pistol. The slide of the Ruger caught al-Bakr on the temple, dazing him.

The assassin remained standing, quickly re-gained his footing, and then slashed at Oz. The pilot ducked, but felt the air churn over his scalp as the blade passed by, ending its arc with a cut to the arm of a Bedouin who had stepped forward to help.

Blinking the blood out of his right eye, Oz clubbed al-Bakr on the back of the head with a quick return swing of his pistol. Though the blow was deadened by the thick turban al-Bakr wore, he was nonetheless knocked unconscious and dropped to the floor of the tent.

The assassin's motionless body was engulfed by

a wave of humanity armed with knives, guns, even scimitars.

One man cried out, "Prince Sulaiman, as the *shaykh* of the Qahidi, I ask that I be allowed to kill this cur that dared break our sacred tradition to harm a guest—"

"No, it must be one of the Tuareg tribe," another interrupted. "Look at his clothes, he tried to pass himself off as one of us."

"That," another alleged, "is why the Banu Hilal tribe should be appointed his executioner."

"Silence!" the prince cried, raising his hands. "Silence!"

The voices fell quiet.

"We will not begin these days of meetings with bloody hands," he said evenly, his piercing eyes mesmerizing those around him. "Take him outside and bind him. He will be tried according to the laws of the Prophet, in an Islamic court. We are not barbarians seeking instant blood vengeance! Each tribe may post a guard if it so chooses."

Two of the Bedouins seized the unconscious assassin, yanked him off the floor, and quickly removed him from the tent.

"Now," Sulaiman announced to the gathered assemblage, "let us go back to our tables and enjoy the meal. We must not let those who would rob us of our celebration succeed."

There was a murmur of agreement as the men sheathed their weapons and returned to the tables.

"And you, my American friend," Sulaiman said, clapping his hand on Oz's muscular shoulder, "I owe you my life." Then he noticed the wound above Oz's eye. "Do you have a medic with you?" he asked solicitiously. "I think your wound needs to be treated."

"Right here." O.T. indicated a member of the Delta Force.

A soldier stepped up to the pilot, studied the freely-bleeding wound a moment, then took out a gauze bandage from his bag. He clamped it over the wound and remarked, "We'll have you repaired as good as new in a moment, Captain."

CHAPTER

10

"Hold it right there!" Newman shouted, threatening the two advancing figures with his pistol.

There was a whispered conversation in Arabic. Newman understood nothing they said, although he did discern the word "American." The two laughed softly and the co-pilot realized that the one with the satchel charge was a woman.

Shit! Newman thought. *How can I shoot a woman?* "Don't come another step closer or I swear I'll shoot," he warned again.

The man on the hill below him said something. Newman recognized one of the words and then realized the man was speaking English.

"Say again, man," Newman said.

"We bring food," the Arab said, this time speaking louder and more slowly. "Food from banquet below."

Bringing food? Newman wondered incredulously. The army airman swore under his breath. What was he going to do now? He didn't want to create an incident, but he didn't want to see the chopper blown to bits by explosives, either.

Wouldn't that look good on his record! "Wait right there and let me see what you've got," Newman demanded.

The co-pilot stumbled down the hill, nearly falling in the loose sand. Because he hadn't had time to mount the NVG on its strap, he was forced to hold it in one hand and his pistol in the other.

"All right, hold still," Newman told the two Arabs standing in front of him. "Now open the basket. Let's see what's in there."

"Open?"

"Yeah, you know, *open*. The basket, man."

The Arab laughed suddenly, finally understanding what the American meant. He reached over to the basket quickly, making Newman lift his pistol ominously.

The Bedouin froze when he saw the pistol leveled at his belly. "It okay," the Arab tried to reassure the nervous American.

The woman lifted the lid on the leather basket and the desert breeze carried the spicy scent of the hot food to Newman's nose.

They must think I'm a damned fool, the co-pilot thought as he holstered his pistol. "Sorry," he said, his trademark grin again overspreading his face. "Thanks a whole lot. It was real nice of you to think of me up here. Here, I'll take it from here."

The woman handed the basket to Newman. "Thanks a lot," he told her again.

"Tea," the man said, handing a hot clay pot to the American. "Me ant tea."

" 'Me ant'?" Newman asked. "Mint tea?"

"Yes, me ant."

Newman chuckled. "I'll take it from here. You go back and join the party. Thanks again," he said with a mixture of embarrassment and relief.

The soldier watched as the two Bedouins climbed down the steep dune. He shook his head and ascended the short distance to his helicopter. "Me ant tea," he chuckled to himself.

He clambered into the chopper, glancing at the scope. What he saw made him forget everything else. A small blip sat atop the hill in the distance opposite the camp.

And then it vanished.

What the hell was that? Newman wondered. The wind and temperature inversions as the desert cooled off made false patterns from time to time, he knew.

He continued to watch the scope for several minutes. Still nothing. Must have just been a wind gremlin, he finally concluded, although he felt uneasy.

He wondered just how far the desert temperature might drop. Already it was almost cool outside the chopper. He eyed the food in the basket he was still holding. It certainly smelled good.

Nope, he told himself. It's better to stick to your cold MREs and stale water. At least maybe you won't be sick tomorrow. He'd been sick enough times that he didn't want to risk it.

Newman examined the scope once more, then opened a cold MRE.

"Soupy, soup, supper time," he grinned to himself.

*   *   *

In the tent below Newman, Oz was again seated at his table. His cut had been only superficial, and although the wound throbbed, it was little more than a nuisance.

"In fact," Oz whispered to O.T. when the gunner inquired about it, "I think it was worth getting. The Bedouins haven't stopped waiting on me all evening!"

O.T. guffawed. "If that's what it takes to win their respect, I think I'll just pass."

Oz felt light-headed and noticed that Ambassador Cookingham's voice sounded a little slurred when he was talking to the prince. In fact, many of the Americans and Bedouins acted as if they were a bit tipsy—an impossibility given the absence of alcohol.

The meal was soon over and the tables cleared. Some of the men produced small drums and several stringed instruments, including an *al-'ud*, a *tanbur*, and a *theorbo*; the latter three instruments looked somewhat like arched-back mandolins or lutes of varying sizes. The performers played several numbers, and many of the Arabs joined in the singing from time to time.

Oz sipped some more of the excellent tea and settled back into the cushions to listen to the music. But the mellow tones of the stringed instruments combined with the languidness the pilot felt, and he soon fell asleep.

He did not awaken again until a heavy weight tumbled onto him. It was Ambassador Cookingham, who had passed out. O.T. and the rest of his crew were asleep, too, Oz noticed with some bewilderment. The pilot sat up groggily and came to a gradual realization—everyone in the room was asleep.

Oz tried to get up but discovered he could only rise to his hands and knees. He lay down again, wishing he could sleep forever. His eyelids drooped as he reached with a leaden hand for the radio pouch fastened to his belt.

With a super effort of will, he forced his hand to inch toward the radio and unsnap the flap on the pouch. He then sluggishly tugged at the radio with fingers that almost refused to function.

Finally he had the radio in his hand. His thumb rested on the power button but the digit refused to move.

The pilot concentrated with all his might on forcing the button down.

In the shadows behind him, a hooded figure rose in the darkness, grasping a *jambiya;* its curved, seven-inch blade inched out of its scabbard. As the Night Stalker struggled to activate his radio, the figure advanced toward him.

The wind was blowing an intolerable amount of dirt into the chopper, and the air was becoming too chilly for comfort. Newman closed the side door of the MH-60K and brushed the dust off his jacket. The night had mercifully cooled down although it was still stuffy inside the aircraft.

Specialist Robert Newman sat down in his bucket seat and realized with some chagrin that he was starting to get sleepy. He toyed with the idea of drinking some of the mint—he corrected himself—"me ant" tea. Surely that wouldn't upset his stomach. The water had undoubtedly been boiled to prepare the tea, so there shouldn't be any microbes lurking about in it to make him ill.

He retrieved the small bottle of tea from the floor of the cockpit and although it now was only lukewarm, he took a few sips of it.

"Not bad," he said aloud.

He lifted the container to his lips and guzzled the whole quart. He wiped a drop off his chin, then screwed the cap back onto the vessel.

So how long does it take caffeine to get into your blood-stream? he wondered with a yawn.

A large blip appeared at the outside range of the radar. Newman sat up and watched the image glide along the edge of the screen. To be that large at that range, he realized, the image just about had to be a formation of several planes.

Probably V-22s, he decided; they were moving too slowly for jets. Perhaps some of the East Sahra military were cruising around on some other mission. The blip vanished from the screen as it left the extreme range of the radar, and Newman decided it was nothing to worry about.

The radio crackled, then was silent. But the channel was clear as if someone were sending a transmission without any data or voice on the carrier wave.

Newman waited five seconds, then toggled the chopper's radio. "Desert Ground, is that you? Say again. Over."

The channel remained open with no answer, just a faint hum. Why wasn't Captain Carson answering his radio?

"Desert Ground, do you read me?" Newman called. "Desert Four calling Desert Ground. Over."

There was still no reply.

Either the captain's radio was broken or else there was real trouble, Newman realized. But either way, the airman knew he had to take further action.

"Radio check, radio check," he called. "Come in Desert Ground. I'm not receiving you here. Over."

There was no answer. He thought about what

to do next. Climbing down to the camp on foot was out; that would leave the chopper unattended.

The wind shook the aircraft as Newman lifted his NVG and inspected the area around the tent. The two Bedouin guards outside the tent were huddled together as if asleep. He shifted his view and checked the Delta Force troops guarding the other MH-60K and the AH-64.

Both guards were slumped over next to the choppers.

"What the hell's going on!" Newman muttered under his breath. He wished he had a pair of binoculars.

He tried to think calmly and rationally.

The airman knew he couldn't leave the chopper unattended. He wondered if there might be someone stalking him this very moment with a silenced weapon. The Bedouins and guards might well be dead rather than asleep, judging from their appearance. His best bet, he decided, would be to get the chopper into the air, try once more to reach the captain, and—if he was still unsuccessful—link to the COMSAT and contact Commander Warner.

Newman realized he wasn't authorized to fly a chopper by himself. SOP required at least a two-man crew before a helicopter could be flown. But more than one military chopper had been operated by a single man during an emergency, and this was *definitely* an emergency.

Newman proceded to perform the functions necessary to activate the engines of the helicopter. As he did so, he saw a movement out of the corner of his eye and glanced toward the camp.

A jeep pulling a trailer had come to a halt in front of the main tent and four Bedouins were climbing out.

The co-pilot swore loudly as he toggled on the radio for one more try at contacting Oz. "Desert Ground, you've got company! Come in please."

Qaim eyed the aircraft on the dune high above them as its blades started chopping at the air.

"Talam, get one of the rifles out of the trailer," he ordered.

His son obediently collected the gun and followed the others into the conference tent.

The wind howled plaintively and Qaim blinked the grit from his eyes as he looked around the huge room. A jumble of bodies lay on the floor of the tent and sprawled across the low tables. The four intruders hesitated at the entrance, almost fearful of walking among the sleeping men.

"Here," a voice called softly in Arabic. "The prince is over here. I have bound him already."

Talam shouldered his rifle and began navigating through the bodies toward the voice.

"It is Habbas," Qaim told the others. "The one we were told to meet." He eyed the sleeping prince and spoke to Habbas, "Why is the prince unconscious?"

"A mistake," Habbas answered. "The cup without the drug went to one of the Americans. Fortunately we were able to replace the flier's drink soon after discovering the error. He finally succumbed— but for a while I thought I was going to have to cut his throat." He was silent a moment and noticed the sound of rotors chopping the air above the camp. "What is that noise outside?" he inquired of Qaim. "Did you come by helicopter?"

"No," Qaim answered. "One of the American choppers is starting. If they decide to stop us, I don't know—"

"A helicopter?" Habbas interrupted. "That is impossible." He stooped to assist Qaim and his sons, who were trying to lift the prince from the floor. "I took the drugged tea to all the guards and the crewman myself."

"Well, at least one of them must not have drunk it," Qaim said as Parim held the flap of the tent open for them.

The Bedouins stepped into the furious storm of stinging sand, crossed to the jeep, and carefully laid the prince's body onto the trailer of provisions.

"Parim, you ride back here, too," Qaim ordered as he covered the prince's face with a loose cloth. "Be sure he doesn't fall," the father instructed, "and keep his face covered so the sand doesn't choke him. Use some of the ropes to secure him into the trailer."

Newman watched helplessly as the jeep pulled away from the camp.

He pulled the collective pitch lever, lifting the chopper from the dune in a flurry of dust and sand that obscured the valley below for a few seconds. The wind whipped the cloud of dust away as the chopper dropped toward the camp.

Newman had planned on calling Commander Warner when he got into the air, but connecting

with the satellite in the sandstorm that was develop-
ing would take time and would be subject to so much
interference that he might not be able to accomplish
anything. Flying high enough to clear the storm
might take even more time and Newman had no idea
of how high a sandstorm might extend into the atmosphere.

Instead of attempting to operate the radio, the
army airman centered the MH-60K over the clearing in front of the meeting tent and pushed on the
collective pitch lever. The chopper dropped, shaking
in the wind, until it bumped into the surface, which
was nearer than Newman had thought in the white-
out. The helicopter bounced on its landing gear,
then settled, rocking in a blast of grit-laden air.

The co-pilot vaulted from the chopper, shield-
ing his eyes against the stinging sand with one hand
as he drew his pistol with the other. He crossed toward the tent, his clothes flapping in the wind. For
a fleeting moment he thought how much the storm
resembled a Colorado blizzard.

The interior of the tent looked like a battle-
ground. Bodies were sprawled all over the floor and,
at first, Newman thought the men were all dead. But
then he noticed that no one appeared to have been
wounded.

Poison gas! Newman surmised, and wondered
how long it would be before he succumbed. Then
he remembered the people in the jeep. They hadn't
been wearing any type of gas masks as far as he could
tell and they didn't seem to have been affected by
any gas.

Newman holstered his pistol, searching the

room for Captain Carson. The wind outside was howling now and the sides of the tent flapped as if the gale were threatening to uproot the structure.

The airman carefully stepped over the still forms on the floor of the tent, searching intently until he located the prone body of his superior. The black co-pilot knelt down beside Oz, who was draped across several cushions and lay next to Ambassador Cookingham.

Newman rolled Oz onto his back and shook the pilot's shoulders. "Captain!" he called.

There was no response.

Feeling a court marshal coming on, the airman slapped Oz's face. "Captain, wake up. We've got trouble."

Oz's eyes fluttered open. "What the hell . . ." he mumbled.

"You've got to wake up, sir. Everybody's been drugged or something. Keep you eyes open!"

"Where are we?" Oz asked lethargically, trying to sit up but failing. He looked around dazedly and then tried to focus on Newman.

"Everybody's been drugged or something, sir," Newman repeated.

Oz tried to stay awake. "Where's the prince?" he whispered.

Newman scrutinized the bodies around him, assuming the prince would be close to Captain Carson and the ambassador. "I don't see him, sir. A bunch of guys came to the tent in a jeep and carried somebody out," the airman said, his worst fears indisputably confirmed.

Oz nodded languidly and closed his eyes; he didn't open them again.

Newman knew then that his superior was going to be of no help. There was only one thing left to do: he had to stop that jeep and get the prince off it. He carefully laid the captain's head back onto the cushion, stepped over the bodies, and headed for the entrance.

12

As the chopper roared over the desert, Newman sat tensely in the helicopter's cockpit, the screens and instruments bathing his face an eerie green. The airman had ceased attempting to contact Commander Warner on the COMSAT; the sandstorm seemed to have blacked out the satellite. The wind buffeted the chopper and pelted it with sand.

Newman took off his NVG; the goggles couldn't penetrate the sandstorm. He left the instrument hanging under his chin from the rubber hose that stretched around the back of his helmet.

The airman studied the rolling hills of the desert's surface through the forward looking infrared scope. The FLIR gave him a fairly good, if somewhat narrow, picture of the surface since the sand was considerably warmer than the nighttime air blowing over it.

A sudden gust shoved the chopper dangerously close to the face of a cliff.

"Time to get a little altitude between you and them," Newman told himself, lifting the collective pitch lever in his left hand. The MH-60K responded smoothly to climb higher.

The airman checked his VSD screen and discovered he was heading back toward the camp. He swore loudly and turned the chopper back onto the proper course.

"Going to have to be careful not to get turned around," he cautioned himself. "Now where's that jeep?"

Newman searched without sighting the jeep for nearly an hour. Then he remembered it had come into camp on the dried creek bed. If it had followed the wash when it left, that would be the logical place to look. He knew scanning the whole desert with the tiny FLIR screen wasn't going to cut it.

Newman tapped a button to the side of his HSD and punched two buttons on his keyboard, carefully watching to be sure he was well above the ground. After consulting the horizontal situation display screen, he hit more keys on the chopper's computer console. "That must be the creek bed there," he said aloud, eyeing the map overlay generated on the HSD by the mission data cartridge in the computer.

The airman kicked the left pedal so the chopper nosed into the direction that would intersect the arroyo and pressed the control column forward. The MH-60K accelerated abruptly, pushing him back into his bucket seat as he hurtled above the surface of the desert. He watched the map overlay of the area on the HSD. Within minutes, the arroyo appeared on it.

He checked the FLIR and saw the creek bed. He eased back on the control column and stomped on the right pedal to align the nose of the chopper. Then he shoved the control column forward again, adjusting it a little to the left to compensate for the wind.

"Now where are you, you suckers?" Newman asked, fighting to suppress a yawn. He wondered when the caffeine from the tea was going to kick in, realizing that if it didn't start working soon, he might fall asleep.

He checked the instruments, then glanced toward the FLIR. The hot points generated by the jeep's engine, exhaust, and the six bodies appeared on the screen.

"Got you now, suckers!" Newman whooped. He lowered the collective pitch lever, dropping the helicopter and matching the speed of the fleeing vehicle below.

The American chopper seemed to materialize over the Bedouins like one of Satan's demons. The machine dropped from the dusty sky and flooded the jeep with light; on the trailer behind the jeep, Parim started screaming like a child.

"Give me a rifle," Qaim ordered Habbas.

The Bedouin handed Qaim one of the old five-shot Mauser rifles they'd found on the trailer.

Qaim jerked the bolt back and checked to be sure it was loaded. The beam from the helicopter revealed the reflection of a brass cartridge. The assassin shoved the bolt closed and rotated the lever to lock the lugs in place. Bracing his legs in the seat and shouldering the weapon, he simultaneously thumbed at the safety to be sure it wasn't engaged. He aimed at the dark shape behind them and fired.

The shot seemed to have no effect. Qaim cycled another round into the firearm's chamber and fired again.

The helicopter dropped closer, its blades whipping up a cloud of dust that engulfed the jeep.

"I can't see!" Kamel screamed from behind the wheel.

"Look out!" Qaim warned, too late.

The vehicle slammed into a boulder, throwing Qaim and Habbas out of the jeep and pitching the others headlong. The helicopter roared overhead, then circled the battered vehicle.

The crash occurred so unexpectedly that Newman laughed out loud at the comic scene below. But as he completed his circle of the impaired vehicle, he yawned again. He pulled back on the control column and kicked the control pedals, enabling the aircraft to be aligned with the jeep while hanging above it.

The remaining three occupants scrambled around to check on the fate of the men in the sand. As Newman watched the FLIR, he noticed that one figure remained stretched out in the open-topped trailer. Was that the prince? the flier wondered.

All right, Newman thought, fighting to keep his eyes open. *Time for a little American rodeo work.*

He checked to be sure there was enough clearance between the cliff faces on either side of the dry creek. Then he lowered the collective pitch lever, dropping the chopper nearly to ground level and kicking up a hurricane of sand.

When it appeared that the chopper was about to drop right on top of them, the Arabs below the aircraft were terrified. The blizzard of sand so blinded the men that, as they tried to evade the deafening roar, they begain colliding with one another and tripping over the rocks.

"Kind of like herding cattle in Colorado," Newman grinned to himself as the five men dispersed in every direction. The airman hovered for a moment above the motionless Bedouin in the trailer who still appeared to be unconscious. The black pilot decided to ignore him for a while and concentrate on the others who were on foot.

He toyed with the idea of arming the machine gun pod but quickly decided he was not justified in firing at the fleeing figures. Instead, he would simply drive them like cattle until they were far enough away that he could double back and get the prince— if that was who was lying unconscious in the trailer behind the jeep.

Newman yawned and lethargically nudged the chopper forward, dropping to within inches of the surface of the arroyo. The MH-60K vacillated in the gale of sand it created, then commenced to chase after the four terrified figures up ahead.

"Up this draw," Qaim directed Habbas and his sons, his burnoose flapping in the downdraft. He could barely discern the split in the cliff face that led upward from the gravelly bed of the dry stream.

"Hurry up," he urged, "the chopper is gaining on us."

As the four men stumbled past and started to climb, Qaim drew the CZ-83 pistol from his robe, recalling the Bedouin story about the man who hunted elephants with a peashooter. He lifted his .32-caliber gun and aimed, trying to envision where the pilot must be sitting in the nose of the craft. Squinting in the bright landing light, the tribesman fired his pistol as fast as he could, emptying it into the nose of the flying monster. He threw his empty weapon at the machine, then turned and clambered up the rock after the others.

"Have to hand it to that guy," Newman laughed sluggishly as the .32-caliber bullets were deflected by the Plexiglass windscreen. "He has more nerve than I'd have with an eight-ton egg beater about to chew my tail!" The airman found himself struggling to stay alert. As he watched the four men on the FLIR scamper like scared rabbits up the cliff and across the open plain, he decided it was time to double back for the prince.

He felt so weak he could hardly push the rudder pedal to get the chopper turned around. His eyelids drooped as he lifted the collective pitch lever. He leaned back into his bucket seat, fighting to stay awake.

Slowly, he slumped forward in the chair, his left hand weighing down the collective pitch lever as his right pushed forward on the control column.

The chopper responded instantly, dropping as it accelerated away from the jeep.

The MH-60K slammed into the side of the opposite cliff, its nose shattering and its rotors beating themselves apart against the sandstone face. The aircraft plunged thirty feet downward to the surface of the arroyo, where one of the fuel tanks ruptured.

Three minutes later, the darkness was briefly turned into daylight as a giant fireball soared into the dust-filled sky.

C H A P T E R

13

From the ridge overlooking the arroyo, Qaim turned toward the explosion of the helicopter. The fireball was barely discernable through the blowing sand as it climbed upward from the burning wreckage into the nighttime sky. *It is like a miracle,* Qaim told himself. Had one of his pistol bullets struck its mark? he wondered. Whatever had happened, the aircraft that had been impervious to bullets a few moments before was now burning.

To his amazement, Qaim watched Talam drop to his knees, oblivious to the gravel that chewed into his legs, and launch into the *Shahada* prayer chant normally led by an Imam. *"Allah-u Akbar, Allah-u Akbar. La illah illa Allah . . ."* he intoned. *"God is most Great, God is most Great, I testify that there is but one God . . ."*

Kamel and Parim joined their brother, and the two young voices became a higher harmony to the droning of the older son's utterance; the words of the *Shahada* were wafted over the ridge and lost in the wind.

Qaim remained standing as the descant continued and the ordnance in the helicopter rocked the dry stream bed with an explosive counterpoint.

Sergeant Marvin thought he had only just fallen asleep in his poncho when he felt himself being shaken.

"Sarge, you've got a message," a voice was saying.

Marvin fought the urge to curse and glared up at the soldier standing over him. "Didn't I tell you not to wake me unless it was an emergency?" he demanded.

"Yes, Sergeant, I was told," Specialist Star stammered. "Rogers told me not to bother you before he went off duty—I'm on the second shift. But it looks like we *do* have an emergency, Sergeant Marvin."

Marvin grumpily got to his feet, brushing the sand off his pants. "Why didn't you say so in the first place!" he groused. "What's the problem?"

"Desert One is a half-hour overdue to check in with us," the soldier confided as they started walking toward the helicopter.

"Didn't you try to reach Captain Carson?" Marvin demanded.

"Yes, sir. And we weren't able to reach anyone at the meeting site."

"Could there be some sort of problem caused by the weather?"

"We thought of that. They *are* having a bad sandstorm to the south of us so they might have had trouble from the ground. But I'm sure Captain Carson would have put a bird in the air in order to check in."

"Yeah, that's true," Marvin agreed. "We'd better get to a COMSAT link. If that doesn't work, we'll check with Commander Warner to see if he wants us to go out to their camp."

Marvin glanced up at the stars twinkling in the desert sky. *Damn it, Oz, what's going on?* he wondered as he opened the side door and climbed into the chopper.

The sandstorm started to diminish as the last of the chopper's ordnance exploded, sending a final shower of sparks and burning debris across the dry floor of the valley. A giant smoke-ring rose from the last explosion, its ghostly circle lit by the flickering blaze of the wreckage. To Qaim, it seemed as if the spirit of the monstrous vehicle had climbed into heaven, leaving its earthly carcass behind.

As they climbed down the rocky slope, they found Habbas, who had slipped while trying to climb the cliff. He lay at the base of the rise, barely discernable in the dim light from the flaming helicopter, draped across a gravel bar.

Qaim knelt by the body, which already felt cold to the touch. The angle of the man's neck made it obvious that it was broken. Qaim rolled Habbas over.

"He is dead," Qaim announced in a low voice barely audible over the crackling of the distant helicopter. "Habbas is dead," he repeated.

They silently crossed toward the jeep and gathered around the unconscious prince still lying on the trailer behind the jeep.

Qaim searched for a pulse on the prince's neck. He discovered the point over the jugular vein and detected a faint beating. "He is alive," he reported to the others.

"Allah be praised," Talam muttered. Like the others, he knew their client had been adamant about the prince remaining unharmed during the kidnapping.

"We are leaking water from the radiator," Kamel called from the front of the jeep.

Only a few beads of water dripped from under the radiator, forming a damp circle in the sand below. But Qaim knew that even a small leak, over time, would spell disaster when the heat of the morning sun came upon them. Even with the extra stores of drinking water that were in the trailer, they would soon be in trouble as the water evaporated into the sand, a few drops at a time.

"We must go as far as we can before it gets warm," Talam urged.

"The wind is dying," Kamel added. "We should be able to make good time now."

"But we can't leave Habbas in the open for the animals of the desert," Parim objected.

"Neither can we take his body with us!" Kamel protested. "It will begin decomposing soon in the hot desert sun."

Qaim eyed the clothing the dead man wore. "We will bury him in a shallow grave," he decided. "In that sand bar over there."

The assassin knew the Americans would discover the wreckage of the nearby helicopter. Since there was no way to cover the jeep's tracks now that the wind had died, they would undoubtedly also find Habbas' grave. If they identified the body, it might be possible for the authorities to track the Bedouin back to Qaim and his family.

They would buy time by making Habbas unrecognizable, Qaim resolved. With luck, the Americans might even mistake the body for that of the prince since both were dressed identically.

Having made his decision, Qaim drew his dagger and approached the inert body.

"Captain Carson!" someone was calling. "Captain Carson."

Oz shook his head, opening heavy eyelids. "What? What's going on!"

"You've been drugged, sir, as nearly as we can tell." Sergeant Marvin was crouched over Oz, shaking him into consciousness. "I had the medic give you and your crew some stimulants," he said. "I know it was risky, but we had to do it. The prince is missing, sir, and so is Desert Four."

Oz sat up, swearing under his breath and rubbing his stiff neck. The tent was now lit by the harsh glare of portable electric floodlights. A Delta Force medic was stepping over the prone men on the floor.

"Is everyone okay?" Oz asked, shakily getting to his feet and glancing at the bodies lying around him.

"Four of the men are dead, sir," Marvin answered. "Three apparently suffocated when they fell asleep outside; the sandstorm nearly covered them.

Another man here in the tent appears to have had a coronary, as near as the medic can tell."

"Damn Mickey Finns!" O.T. muttered, crossing over to Oz. "I thought Bedouins never harmed their guests," he added sarcastically.

"They wouldn't do this," Ambassador Cookingham insisted in a groggy voice. "Outsiders must be responsible."

"Or someone who's very desperate," O.T. said.

"The missing chopper—what happened to it?" Oz asked.

"Newman was on duty, sir," Marvin answered. "He called on the first radio check with us. But he never called in on the next check. That's what alerted us that there might be a problem out here. We got in touch with Commander Warner and he ordered us to fly over here ASAP. Newman's missing—along with the chopper."

"That's strange," Oz said. "I seem to remember him being here with us in the tent after we'd been drugged. I tried to reach him by radio but could only switch it on. I don't know, I might have just imagined it, but I thought he said something about the prince and there being a jeep."

"If there was a jeep," Marvin said, "the winds that developed would have erased its tracks. But I have to wonder if Newman followed whoever kidnapped the prince."

"Perhaps there was something seriously wrong with the prince, and Newman flew him back to Bhaliq," Ambassador Cookingham suggested.

"Not without contacting someone," Oz answered. "If he'd done that, he would have radioed

Marvin or Commander Warner. No, I'm betting he followed the plane or vehicle of whoever came in and snatched the prince. How soon's daylight?" Oz asked, checking his watch.

"About two hours," Marvin answered. "The medics think everyone should come around by then."

"Let's get things rounded up so we can start a search with first light," Oz said. "We'll make this area our command center and search outward from it. Have you informed the king of what happened?"

Marvin shook his head. "No, sir."

"That's my job," Ambassador Cookingham sighed. "A job I don't relish," he added, shaking his head.

C H A P T E R

14

As the sun cleared a distant sandstone cliff, Oz raised the MH-60K into the desert sky. The heat created ghosts of hot air that shimmered and danced in waves while the nocturnal insects and snakes retreated from the light into cracks and holes in the desert floor. Oz circled the camp to align the chopper on its course, the purple sunrise taking on a pink and orange tint that burned away the darkness on the cliffs and in the valley below.

The clumps of welwitschia and singed grass lost their violet shadings, and the boulders took on the scarlet glow of the morning. The colors of the desert mingled along the gullies and the cracked earth; a warm breeze bred dust clouds that glowed like fog in the burgeoning light.

Ambassador Cookingham bought the Americans some needed time. First, he talked the king into waiting before taking any action against the Qahidi, Sa'adi, or Banu Hilal tribes since it was uncertain that they were involved in the kidnapping. Second, the ambassador managed to wring an agreement from the Bedouins at the conference; they were to remain at the conference for three days on the contingency that Prince Sulaiman could be returned.

Oz divided the area around the camp into quadrants, giving Desert Six and the now-repaired Desert Three the northern quadrants closest to Bhaliq.

"We'll have to be really careful," Oz told the pilots of the other two choppers during a short briefing. "Some of these tribes are armed to the teeth since they've been preparing for civil war."

"Any idea exactly how much armament the tribes might possess?" Lieutenant Rivera asked.

"The Bedouins have had centuries of experience moving goods in and out of the desert," Oz answered. "They'd be experts at smuggling weapons. According to some CIA reports Ambassador Cookingham has seen, we could encounter armor and various types of anti-aircraft weapons. And the jury's still out on where the Mirage jets came from that attacked us yesterday."

Oz informed the two pilots that one squad of Delta Force would be left behind to guard the peace conference site; the two remaining squads were to go with the MH-60Ks to help in the air search. If either of the choppers was to locate the prince, a rescue was to be initiated if the situation dictated.

"The worst part of it," Oz continued, "is that any vehicles could be getting farther away from the camp about as fast as we can extend our grid search outward. The longer we take to find the prince, the greater the chance of failure, since we'll have to cover an ever-greater area."

"What about Desert Four?" asked the pilot of the Apache.

"I'm assuming for now that it has been downed," Oz answered. "Otherwise, we would have heard from Newman. But even if it has been destroyed, it could point the direction to the kidnappers. So keep a sharp lookout for any wreckage."

Within minutes, the three American helicopters were airborne. Oz took his crew to the south, ferrying a half-full fuel bladder below the chopper to preclude a return to camp for refueling. The other two choppers would be refueled from the fuel tanks that a squadron of V-22s were to bring in within several hours, at which point the East Sahran military would also join in the search.

Along with a sweaty squad of Delta Force troopers sitting in the passenger compartment of Oz's chopper was a single Bedouin tribesman named Mahmoud Jaber. A soft-spoken, heavy-set mountain of bone and muscle, Jaber was to serve as the group's interpreter if the Americans needed to interrogate any Bedouins as they searched the desert.

Like the other choppers, the crew of Desert One was to follow a carefully-worked grid search throughout the day. As he scanned the desert below, Oz found himself worrying about what the consequences might be of having lost the prince. The pilot had been personally responsible for the man's safety; more than one military career had ended under such a cloud.

He chided himself for having put so much stock in the assurances of both the prince and ambassador that the Bedouins would do nothing to harm a guest. If there was one thing he had learned, it was that people all over the world were abandoning their traditions and taboos. The mistake could be very costly in terms of human life and his career.

As noon approached, O.T. spoke over the intercom. "There's something on the port side. Looks like wreckage, but it might be a vehicle hunkered down in the heat."

Oz kicked his left pedal so the helicopter turned toward port. "Yeah, I see it," the pilot said, squinting in the sunlight. "We'd better go in and take a look."

He circled the vehicle cautiously. It proved to be an ancient half-track, possibly left over from World War II; the wind had chipped and sanded it away to expose bare metal. The tires at the front were rotted into piles of black rubber that lay around the wheel rims. One of the tracks had been thrown, apparently stranding the occupants decades before.

The crew and passengers of the MH-60K needed a break from their cramped quarters, and because it was nearly time to refuel, Oz descended near the half-track, raising a cloud of dust as he lowered the fuel bladder and then landed. Within minutes, however, they were airborne again, continuing their search. Oz landed twice more to check several caves and to refuel.

The fiery day wore on and evening approached without any clue as to the fate of the prince or the missing chopper. Oz contacted the commander in charge of the East Sahran air search; he, too, had had no success. The pilot then called for a final progress check of the American helicopters: "Desert Three, this is One. See anything? Over."

"That's a negative, Desert One," the tired voice of Lieutenant River answered.

"Nothing, One," the pilot of the AH-64 answered a few minutes later.

"Return to the camp," Oz ordered the chopper pilots. "We'll check in every four hours. Over."

"That's a roger, Desert One. Desert Six is heading in to call it a day. Over and out."

Majid Qaim and Talam lay on their bellies on the rocky outcrop, peering over the ridge toward the squalid camp that blocked their path.

"You see," Talam told his father, "it will be impossible to pass this way."

"Yes," Qaim concurred. "We can not get around that camp if we stick to the arroyo. They've managed to plant themselves in the one clear spot in this range of steep cliffs."

"We could retrace our steps," Talam suggested.

"That would set us behind by half a day or more," Qaim objected. "The jeep won't last that long, even if the Americans don't overtake us. They almost had us an hour ago when they passed."

"Should we wait for nightfall and sneak past the camp on foot?" Talam asked.

"No. Let's drive right into the camp and trade the jeep for some donkeys or dromedaries. They seem to have a wealth of animals. You can make another temporary patch for the jeep's radiator; that should hold long enough for us to make the swap. There's lots of gasoline left so the tribesmen should be interested. We can be far away before they discover they've been tricked."

Talam said nothing. Tricking fellow Bedouins, even if they were of a different tribe, sounded distasteful to him.

By setting up a temporary camp, Desert One would be able to get a quick start the next day when the search continued. Their lodging was to be an old fort that Oz had noted on their data cartridge before he briefed the other chopper pilots.

The bleached stones of the fortress glowed pink in the sunset. The foundation of the fort had been laid during the 1930s when the French Foreign Legion had sought to extend its influence across Morocco and into the Sahara. Fort Danjou was manned mostly by Americans and Englishmen who had been forced by the depression of the 1930s to become French Legionnaires.

During a bloody skirmish against the charismatic Bedouin leader Abd el-Krim, the soldiers in the fort were slaughtered to a man. The French government then abandoned Fort Danjou to the desert creatures, with only an occasional tourist or nomad visiting the site since its downfall.

Oz and his men carefully inspected the stronghold from the air. A dune was attempting to scale the thirty-foot eastern walls, and the roofs of the barracks and storage rooms had long since collapsed. The front gate had vanished, probably having become fuel for the campfires of passing caravans.

"I'm taking us down," Oz told his crew. "Sergeant Young."

"Yes, sir," answered the leader of the Delta Force squad over the intercom.

"We're headed in. Have your squad spread out immediately in case we run into any trouble."

"Yes, sir."

The helicopter settled into the wide courtyard of the camp. As the American soldiers leaped from the aircraft and quickly secured the walls of the old fortress, a bandit scout watched intently from a distant cliff.

"Come nightfall," the scout smiled to himself as he returned his scratched telescope to its leather case, "we will have plunder brought in by the foreigners." He rose to his feet, oriented himself with the evening star that now was bright in the west, and headed back to his camp.

CHAPTER

15

"With any luck," Qaim was saying, "the Americans will find Habbas's body, assume it is the prince, then track the jeep to the Qahidi camp and wipe it out." He laughed lightly, happier now that they had succeeded in trading their jeep and supplies for five dromedaries and two Arabian camels.

"That should be quite a fight," he added, "with the weapons the Qahidi have squirreled away in their tents. Did you notice their faces when I warned them about American helicopters attacking Bedouins?" He smiled. "They'll open fire the minute they see an American aircraft!"

Talam said nothing, finding the whole idea abhorrent.

Qaim bounced along on top of the dromedary that he rode next to the prince. Not having been astride one of the beasts since he was a child, the assassin had forgotten how uncomfortable the high-backed saddle could be. He turned to study his three sons who rode behind him, looking ill at ease but doing better than he had expected, especially considering the way Parim's beast had bitten and spit at the young man when he had mounted.

"Let him know who is the master," Qaim had advised the youth, striking the woolly-haired beast in the head with the barrel of his rifle. The blow created a cut that oozed for hours. But the camel didn't attempt to bite anyone again.

The few supplies they had needed—food, water, and three meager tents—were unloaded from the trailer and placed on the packs tied to the two Arabian camels. The pack animals, like the other members of the *Camelidae* family, seemed to have no desire to work. They whined when the pack was mounted and grunted and groaned loudly when forced to their feet to begin the journey. Once the trip commenced, however, they plodded along without further complaint.

Now the five Bedouins rode across the blistering sand, sitting motionless to conserve energy and avoid creating muscular heat. Each of the riders carried two gallon-cans of water. The prince rode bound and unarmed, not speaking to anyone. Qaim and each of his sons had a Mauser rifle slung alongside their saddles. The two riderless camels followed.

Qaim checked the compass he'd torn from the dashboard of the jeep as well as the setting sun and ascertained that they were still traveling in the right direction. Although they moved more slowly on camel than they would have in the jeep, they followed a more direct route.

"We should be about halfway there," the assassin announced to the others. "We'll stop in the valley up ahead and camp for the night in that clump of vegetation."

"An oasis?" Kamel asked.

"No," Qaim replied. "Too far from any mountains or tall hills for an oasis." It amazed Qaim how little his sons knew about the desert. In one generation, they had become city dwellers rather than true *badawis.* "The vegetation will be dry and dead when we arrive, you can wager on that. It won't green until the next brief rainfall."

"Then we could build a fire," Parim said, his body swaying with the camel's gait. "I could use a good hot meal."

"No fires," Qaim interrupted. "There are bands of robbers in this area, and the Americans may continue their search through the night, although I doubt they have the manpower to do so. But we're not taking any chances. We will eat our meal cold tonight."

The sunset cast long shadows across Fort Danjou. The cracked wall and broken stones piled in the corners of the fort appeared to reshape themselves into ghostly outlines as the light grew dimmer. A breeze rustled the sand, and a spiny-tailed lizard scampered across the gravel, making a disconcerting racket.

"You can almost imagine the ghosts of the dead Legionnaires encircling this fort," Luger mused quietly. The gunner, O.T., Mahmoud Jaber, and one of the Delta troopers, Private John Zeller all ate their MREs. O.T. and Zeller were in the open side door of the MH-60K, their legs dangling over the ground. Luger and Jaber sat in the sand.

"Keep talking about ghosts and you'll spook everybody," O.T. told Luger. "I remember hearing about a soldier in 'Nam whose patrol found a nice dry Buddhist temple to stay in during an overnighter. Somebody told a ghost story and the whole squad got so jumpy they had to spend the night outside—in the rain!"

"You're kidding," Luger laughed.

"Nope," O.T. insisted. "I got soaked to the bone."

Luger and the others laughed heartily.

"Guess I'll keep my morbid thoughts to myself," the gunner chuckled. "Although I doubt we'd have to stand in the rain tonight."

Oz was approaching the helicopter from across the courtyard. "O.T., Luger," he said as he neared the group. "You guys mind sleeping on board the chopper tonight? I'd like to have you close by to man the Miniguns if we should need some firepower."

"No problem," O.T. answered. "Between the cold and the scorpions, I'd as soon stay in the 'copter anyhow."

"Me, too," Luger agreed, screwing the lid back onto his canteen.

"Good. Keep the side doors locked and your NVGs handy. I'll either be up front in the chopper or have a hand-held radio with me if I'm outside. I'll have your helmet mikes tied into the helicopter's radio."

"Sounds good," O.T. replied.

"Mr. Jaber," Oz addressed the Arab translator, "could you stay on board tonight, too?"

"Certainly, no problem," the Bedouin answered.

"Okay, thanks. I'll see you guys later," Oz said, moving off on his final rounds. He checked on the Delta Force soldiers settling in for the night, some of whom were preparing to sleep inside the shell of an old stone stable. At either entrance of the roofless structure, the squad's FN Minimi machine guns rested on their bipods, prepared for action at a moment's notice.

The soldiers on the first watch carried M203 grenade launchers; the men were not assigned to fixed positions but would continue to move along the fortress walls, much as their French Legionnaire counterparts had decades before.

"How's it going, Sergeant Young?" Oz asked, approaching the soldier responsible for security.

"Well, sir," the Tennessean drawled, "we've got clear fields of fire around the fort. I don't much like that cliff overlooking the camp," he said pointing, "but we have it covered with a Minimi. We've set Claymores along the walls, and the guards are all equipped with hand-held radios and NVGs. Nobody's going to sneak up on us tonight, sir."

"Good," Oz said. "I'm going to get a little shut eye. But don't hesitate to contact me if you need to."

"I won't, sir. Good night."

"Good night."

*　　*　　*

"We would stand a much better chance of finding the prince if we utilized *all* our V-22s," General Mahala urged the king.

"We will not throw our entire fleet of aircraft into the search," King Khadduri remarked acidly to the officer standing before him. "We'll let the Americans continue for a few more days. Just be sure the news reporters have the details about the abduction of my son." The king sat behind an ornately carved Moroccan desk in the palace room from which he conducted most of his business.

"But the Americans have only three helicopters," Mahala objected, gesturing with enough force to make the medals on his uniform jangle. "And we've committed just five of our aircraft to the search. There's almost no way they can cover the desert."

The king slapped an ivory letter-opener onto his desk and glared at the military officer standing before him. "You know that if we commit our full forces to the search, we will leave ourselves wide open to an attack on Bhaliq," he barked. "Besides, Ambassador Cookingham has assured me that one of the U.S. spy satellites will be positioned to help in the search during the next few days."

"But your majesty," Mahala countered incredulously, "those satellites can only observe what's in the open. In a day or two, the kidnappers will probably have the prince hidden so well that—"

"The Americans lost him," the king interrupted petulantly. "Now, we let them find him! I want to hear no more about it." He rose, straightened his robes, and prepared to retire from the room.

The general said nothing more about committing additional planes to the search, knowing that to press the issue would be futile and might provoke the sovereign's wrath. He bowed as the monarch and his bodyguard turned to leave.

The Bedouin leader stopped, faced the military officer, and spoke to him kindly. "Don't worry, Ali," he said. "I am certain that this will work out for the best." Then he turned away and crossed the marble tile to the baroque side entrance.

The armed guard standing at the door opened it smartly, then snapped to attention as the king and his bodyguard exited.

General Mahala stood for a moment, mulling over the odd conversation.

Something wasn't right, he knew. King Khadduri wasn't responding to the crisis properly.

Mahala left the room deep in thought, trying to decide what could be done to find the prince and thereby avert a civil war.

Aslam's thin, swarthy face was deeply lined from extensive periods spent in the desert sun. The bandit leader's dark eyes gleamed in the light from the campfire around which his men sat, roasting chunks of lamb skewered by knives or swords. "So there is a helicopter?" he finally asked.

"Yes, only one helicopter," Hasan the scout nodded, rubbing the large mole on his scarred forehead. "At least twelve, perhaps fifteen, soldiers climbed out of the aircraft. With machine guns," he added, wanting to be certain his leader fully understood the dangers.

"Machine guns," Aslam repeated, pulling at his lip. Although he hated to risk his men to the overwhelming fire power the strangers might possess, overrunning the camp and capturing the machine guns, not to mention whatever they could strip from the helicopter, made extra risks worth considering. "How are the men deployed in the fort?" he asked.

Hasan licked his lips and gestured as he spoke. "I saw five standing guard on the walls. They were wearing contraptions on their faces and moving about constantly. It will be impossible to predict where they will be at any given time since they shift around so. And they have strung devices on wires along the walls."

"Explosives," suggested one of the bandits next to the fire.

"Do they have guards inside the fort as well?" Aslam asked around the kabob he popped into his mouth.

"I do not believe so," Hasan responded. "I suspect that most of the men are sleeping in the old stable—though it is hard to see from the cliff overlooking the fort."

"Did they find the tunnel?" Aslam asked, leaning forward eagerly.

"No," the scout grinned, exposing the gap where his front teeth should have been. "It is covered with sand. The soldiers walked right over it but failed to notice."

Aslam stood up, casting a long shadow that flickered in the light of the campfire. His band of men had surprised more than one traveler taking sanctuary in the fort. "So they are ours," he laughed aloud.

"Get the Saracen ready," he ordered the two brigands who served as mechanics for the armored car they'd stolen from the East Sahran Military. "Tonight we will draw infidel blood," Aslam vowed, "and enjoy the booty that has dropped into our snare."

16

"Give me room," Hasan growled at the malefactor behind him as they made their way thought the spider-infested tunnel. Since Hasan toted the single torch, the line of twenty outlaws stretching into the darkness behind kept crowding forward.

The torch he carried was less than ideal, consisting of a thick club of wood with rags soaked in camel's fat wrapped around one end. It burned with a flickering yellow flame that created foul-smelling black soot. Hasan held the light high in the narrow tunnel to keep the smoke away from his face.

The tunnel had been constructed by Arab engineers working for Abd el-Krim more than half a century earlier, the lumber for it having been hauled on the backs of camels and slaves from the nearest oases.

The French Legionnaires thought Fort Danjou was impregnable. But one night—much like tonight, Hasan mused, as he crouched to avoid bumping into a low beam—the Bedouins had stealthily emerged from the tunnel into the middle of the fort's courtyard. The desert warriors had slaughtered most of the foreigners before the soldiers had even known they were under attack.

Finally Hassan reached the crude wooden ladder at the end of the tunnel. "Stand back while I open the trapdoor," he warned the others. He knew he would needed plenty of room to back up in order to avoid the heavy door when it swung open under the weight of the sand above. Hasan cautiously climbed the ladder.

Oz found he was too keyed up—worried, really—to sleep. He leaned against the MH-60K, staring at the stars in the cloudless sky and wishing he had a cigarette, although he'd stopped smoking a year ago. He was uneasy about what the consequences might be of having lost the prince; he continued to feel personally responsible for the man's safety.

Once before, he'd been concerned that his career might be headed downward. Only then it had been Sandy's fault. His former wife hadn't been an ideal officer's spouse, to say the least. Far from it, really. He thought back to the Christmas party Commander Warner had hosted. Sandy was drinking too much as usual and flirting with Oz's friends, making everyone feel uncomfortable.

The worst of it occurred right before Oz took her home.

"I still maintain that the .45 auto is a better cartridge," O.T. had said, continuing his on-going friendly argument with Luger about what the best pistol cartridge was. The two of them were sitting on a wide overstuffed couch.

"Well, you have more pops with a good nine-millimeter," Luger countered. "If you ever run into more than seven—"

"You army jocks," Sandy suddenly interrupted, leaning over them precariously and sloshing some of her drink onto the carpet. "All you ever talk about is guns. Don't you guys get enough sex, or what?"

The whole room grew silent.

"How 'bout it gals," Sandy demanded, looking around, "isn't that all they ever talk about? Guns and killing. Join the army, see the world, and kill some gooks before they kill you!"

Oz took her by the elbow, an angry blush creeping up his neck. "I think we'd better call it a night, Sandy," he said quietly.

"Afraid I'll get too close to the truth?" she asked, slurring her words.

Everyone tried to ignore the couple as they left, wanting to avoid embarrassing Oz any more than he already was.

Sandy still weighed heavily on his mind partly because he knew that her outrageous behavior stemmed from a desperate fear that he would be killed. He straightened up and walked toward the stone stable where the Delta Force had bedded down in their sleeping bags. If he was going to be awake, he might as well check and make sure that everything was in order.

A scraping sound attracted the pilot's attention: metal brushing against stone, then a dull thud. He searched the darkness. Silhouetted against the sky above the walkway was a man in flowing robes.

Was it Mahmoud Jaber? Oz wondered. He'd

thought the interpreter was in the chopper, but maybe he'd been mistaken.

The pilot jerked his radio out of its belt pouch and thumbed it on to check with Death Song, who was sitting watch in the cabin of the MH-60K.

Before he could utter a word, a hooded man seemed to materialize from nowhere in the gloom in front of him. He slashed at the American with a long, curved scimitar that sliced into the radio, narrowly missing the pilot's fingers.

Oz's pistol was in his hand before he realized he'd even drawn it. He jumped aside to avoid a lunge from the attacker and pulled the trigger.

The shot shattered the silence of the gloomy night, spitting flame that lit the assailant's face. At the moment the bullet impacted, a dark hole appeared in the intruder's head and the man dropped into the black cavity looming in front of Oz.

"We're under attack!" Oz shouted, blinking at the after-image of the dying man etched on his retina.

The stable where the Delta Force was encamped exploded in activity. Soldiers leaped from their bedrolls and struggled to ready their weapons. From the walkways along the walls, automatic weapons bathed the camp with frontal and enfilade fire.

All the guards must be dead! Oz realized. He brought up the NVG from around his neck and looked through them. The walls were suddenly lit in shades of green and white by the night vision goggles. The pilot took careful aim at the rifleman he now saw in the shadow of the wall. He discharged the Ruger P-85 he held and the gunman tumbled to the ground.

Oz spun toward the hole in the middle of the courtyard to see another of the intruders climbing out. The pilot double-tapped his trigger and the Arab dropped back into the dark aperture. The American stepped up to the hole, peered in, and jerked back quickly at what he saw. A fraction of a second later, a bandit climbing the wooden ladder discharged his rifle at the American pilot.

Oz reached into his vest and jerked out a "flash bang" grenade. Although a fragmentation grenade would have been just the ticket, the flash bang would work, he thought. He awkwardly pulled the pin from the grenade while still holding his pistol, and dropped the explosive device down the hole.

He was rewarded with much cursing in Arabic. Three seconds later, the explosion shook the camp, brilliantly lighting the air above the opening.

Heavy gunfire rained down from the walkways as the vandals on the wall targeted the Americans.

Hearing footsteps racing toward him, Oz whirled around, his pistol at the ready.

"Delta!" the soldier yelled and Oz returned his attention to the hole.

"What've you got?" the soldier shouted over the erupting gunfire. Bullets kicked plumes of sand around the two Americans.

"Tunnel," Oz answered. "Got any frags?"

"Yeah," the soldier said. He drew a grenade from his combat vest, pulled the pin, and threw it into the hole. "Grenade!" he yelled.

Moments before the device exploded, another

ruffian peered out of the hole and Oz's pistol discharged into the bandit's neck. The man dropped from sight as the mouth of the tunnel exploded, throwing fragments of iron, wood, and flesh into the air.

The sand next to Oz dropped away as the tunnel beneath him collapsed, and the pilot quickly jumped aside. Bullets continued to crack over his head.

"Get the gunman on the wall," he yelled to the soldier next to him. When there was no response, Oz glanced over at the man, who was now lying on his back, a large wound glistening in the center of his chest.

Knowing there was nothing he could do for the trooper, Oz sprinted toward the chopper. The aircraft needed to be moved away from the crossfire and into the air where the Night Stalkers could counter-attack with the weapons the MH-60K carried.

A Minimi machine gun fired from the stable, sending bullets ricocheting with angry whines along the wall opposite Oz. The pilot continued to discharge his 9mm pistol in the direction of the gunfire pouring into the camp from the walls.

As Oz neared the chopper, a grenade from an M203 exploded in front of it.

One of the ruffians on the wall had fired a captured grenade launcher into the fort but had failed to aim it properly. Bits of sand thrown by the blast stung Oz's face. He ducked under the Minigun at the left of the chopper as Luger swung it around.

The six-barreled weapon fired, the separate discharges from each muzzle creating a rending roar.

Hot brass cascaded from the chute under the firearm, falling into the sand.

The chopper's twin engines were whining to life and its rotors beginning to turn as Oz scrambled into his seat.

"I started her up," Death Song shouted, leaning toward the pilot to be heard over the engine and gunfire. "I figured you'd want to get the chopper out of this."

"You better believe it!" Oz yelled back as another M203 grenade exploded outside. The pilot frantically jabbed the cord from his helmet into the intercom receptacle.

"Whoever's on the wall is getting the hang of using the launcher," Death Song cautioned the pilot over the now-functioning phones in Oz's helmet. "Our weapons pods are armed."

"I'm taking her up," Oz shouted over the intercom, warning his crew as he lifted the collective pitch lever.

Aslam sat inside the turret on the ten-ton, six-wheeled armored Saracen. His hand rested on the grip of a 7.62mm machine gun whose barrel jutted outside the protective armor. Inside, along either side of the vehicle, sat eight of his men, each of whom manned one of the Enfield L70 automatic rifles that had been in the vehicle when they had stolen it from the military.

The driver of the armored personnel carrier drove it poorly since the lack of fuel and spare parts forced the bandits to run the Saracen only when it was absolutely necessary. Normally the vehicle sat in a nearby cave, hidden from the infrequent airplanes that passed overhead.

Upon hearing the first shots in the camp, Aslam had ordered his driver forward. Now the engine belched thick smoke as it raced through the open front gate of the fort.

"Aim at the muzzle flashes on the ground," Aslam ordered his men as the vehicle thundered to a stop in the courtyard. A hailstorm of projectiles bouncing off the armor of the Saracen prevented him from giving any further directives.

The bandit leader's attention was focused on the chopper in the center of the courtyard. The aircraft rose a few feet off the ground as Aslam acquired it in his sights.

He pulled the trigger, determined to keep the booty-laden machine from escaping. The tracers of his machine gun became a river of red fire cutting through the nighttime sky, stitching across the skin of the MH-60K and striking the gunner standing behind his Minigun. Aslam smiled as the gunner dropped out of sight.

The chopper continued to rise, its other Minigun chewing up bandits on the walls. Only then did it dawn on Aslam how heavily the chopper was armed and how soon the battle would turn against him.

"Quick!" he screamed at the driver. "Get us away from that helicopter."

"What?" the driver yelled, the bullets hammering into the metal armor around him, making it impossible to hear.

Aslam slid down from his turret seat to crouch

next to the driver. "Get us out of here!" he shrieked into the man's ear.

As the MH-60K lifted, O.T. cleaned the bandits off the wall with short bursts from his Minigun. The tracers and muzzle blast lit up the wall like distant lightning as the projectiles reached their targets. The last bandit collapsed to the walkway as the helicopter cleared the fort, his body riddled by .30-caliber projectiles.

Oz heard a groan over the intercom as he circled the camp. "Everyone okay back there?" he asked anxiously.

"I'm all right," O.T. answered, then he muttered a long oath.

"What's wrong?" Oz asked.

"Luger's down," O.T. explained. "Is it okay to leave my post to check on him?"

"Yes," Oz replied, dipping the nose of the chopper to fire a blast at a desperado dashing across the open courtyard below. "Death Song, ready the TOW for that APC." The pilot wheeled his helicopter to the north, locating the fleeing Saracen which was bouncing along at nearly forty miles per hour.

"How's Luger?" Oz called back to O.T.

"He's bad. Chest wound. But I think I'm getting the bleeding stopped. Jaber's taken a small hit, too, but he seems to be in pretty good shape."

"We won't need you on the gun for a while," Oz told his warrant officer. "Stay with Luger."

"Roger."

"Death Song," Oz said, "I think we're in range for the TOW."

"We're in range," Death Song agreed.

"Fire when ready."

Death Song grasped the pull-out controls, zeroed the Saracen in his sights, and fired.

Oz held the helicopter on course as the TOW was coughed from its launch tube. A fraction of a second later, there was a puff of smoke as the rocket engine ignited. The projectile sped after the vehicle, Death Song adjusting his joystick controls to keep it on target.

Below them, the Saracen turned to avoid a tall dune looming in its headlights. Death Song kept the APC centered on his screen.

The missile struck.

The APC was torn apart as the TOW rocket collided with its engine, riddling its fuel tank with metal fragments. In just a microsecond a secondary explosion of the fuel vapors flashed through the vehicle and split its heavy armor open as if it was a tin can.

Oz circled the burning vehicle as he slowed to return to the fort. The down draft from the chopper's blades made huge swirls of the black smoke coming from the Saracen.

"There's a group on the ground at three o'clock," Death Song alerted Oz.

"I see them," the pilot replied. He threw the helicopter to the right in a steep bank, skimming a sand hill.

The desperadoes were running in the darkness, but they were clearly exposed in the FLIR by their heat signature against the sand. The pilot's thumb hit the fire button on the control column.

The dual machine gun in the weapon pod showered the desert with lethal projectiles. Oz watched the FLIR screen as he pulled back on the control column, slowing the chopper until it matched the speed of the fleeing ruffians.

He bathed them in a stream of bullets, continuing to fire until all six had fallen headlong into the sand. Then he fired a final burst to ensure that all were dead.

The pilot rotated the helicopter toward the fort and shoved forward on the control column, increasing the pitch of the four main blades for maximum speed. As he skimmed over the desert floor, he had a single goal: to get medical assistance for Luger.

But he was also under orders to continue his search for the prince. The pilot would be forced to return to the fort and make do with the medic there, although he would have preferred to fly his gunner straight to the hospital in Bhaliq.

A chest wound was, Oz knew, almost always serious. So there was no time to waste. "Contact the East Sahran forces on the radio," he instructed Death Song. "Maybe they can send out a medical team or at least supply dust off for our wounded."

17

As he approached the fort, Oz swooped down on another small cluster of bandits firing around the corner of the open front gate. The four manned a .30-caliber Browning which they frantically tried to aim at the chopper as it thundered down on them.

The American pilot thumbed his fire button and observed all four drop as he passed over.

Inside the fort, Sergeant Young was screaming at the machine gunner with the Minimi. "Hit that jerk on the wall! Where the hell's Zeller?"

"Here, Sarge!" the private called, running forward to crouch by the pocked wall next to his superior.

"Take that new sniper rifle and nail that prick to the wall!" he said, pointing at the Arab's position. "He's really hunkered in there and we can't get to him with that machine gun."

"I'll get him, Sarge," Keller promised. The Oklahoma farmboy shouldered his rifle, which sported a standard M16 lower coupled to an Insight Systems' upper receiver; a Douglas target barrel was free-floated in its handguard and an AN/PVS-4 night vision scope was mounted to the rail-topped receiver.

Zeller carefully rested his rifle against the stone ledge, coolly peering through the scope and ignoring the bursts from the nearby Minimi. He saw the muzzle flash as the sniper fired at a Delta Force trooper racing across the courtyard toward the safety of the stone stable.

The soldier was half carrying a wounded comrade who had been lying out in the open. The sniper's three-round burst cut into both men, spilling them into the sand.

"Now I've got you, you bastard," Zeller muttered, aligning the cross hairs of his scope on the sniper's head, which was barely visible above the stone wall.

The American snapped the safety of his rifle downward, engaging the tAP set trigger. He held his breath as his forefinger brushed the trigger and the Insight Systems rifle discharged.

The high-velocity bullet smashed into the bandit's skull, ripping into tiny shrapnel as it exploded through his brain.

"Any others?" Zeller asked, lowering his scope.

Sergeant Young cautiously searched the walls for other stragglers, the dark corners of the area clearly visible to him with the NVG he utilized. He saw no one.

"Cease fire!" he hollered to the Minimi gunner.

The few remaining Delta Force soldiers immediately stopped shooting. Outside the fort they heard a burst from the helicopter as it roared above the installation, clearing away the last of the attackers.

"Be careful of snipers," Young warned his men. "Transfer the wounded into that area over there," he said, pointing. "Where's the medic?"

"Here, Sarge," a sober-looking nineteen-year-old answered from the darkness.

"Take care of American troops first," Young ordered.

"Will do," Private Neal replied, kneeling next to the nearest wounded soldier. He broke his medical field-kit open and laid it on the sand.

Sergeant Young's radio crackled to life. "Desert Ground One, this is Desert Wind. It looks clear out here. How are things going inside? Over."

Sergeant Young gently lowered a wounded soldier to the sand and retrieved his radio from his belt. "It's all clear in here," he answered. "We've aced the last of the attackers."

"I'm coming down," Oz called back. "We've got two wounded on board, one in real bad shape."

"We'll keep the courtyard clear for you to land."

"Thanks, Desert Ground. We've contacted a V-22 that's nearby. They're being dispatched to us to offer medical assistance and to transfer the wounded to Bhaliq. Over and out."

That's good, Young thought, looking around, *because our medic down here's pretty overworked.*

There was no doubt in Oz's mind that Luger was very seriously wounded. The question was whether or not the young gunner would make it back to Bhaliq alive.

The V-22 was already loaded with three dead

and five wounded Delta Force soldiers. The pilot watched helplessly as Neal fastened another plasma container to the tube leading into the vein in Luger's arm. The medic nodded to the two East Sahran soldiers who then carried the injured airman to the waiting plane.

Neal spoke quietly to Oz. "I think he must have serious internal bleeding. I did what I could, but—"

"You did fine," Oz reassured the young man. "That's all anyone could ask of you."

The pilot watched as his unconscious gunner was lifted aboard the V-22. The doors of the craft were closed and the airplane took off, its twin rotors whipping up a cloud of dust as it rose into the starry sky.

The American pilot observed the plane as it ascended, its lights strobing while its blades rotated forward for maximum speed as it shot toward Bhaliq.

"I hope he makes it," O.T. said, quietly standing next to Oz in the darkness.

"Yeah," the pilot agreed, thinking of the scrapes the young gunner had survived with the chopper team. Luger possessed a youthful optimism that often offset the hard-bitten pessimism of the older members of the team. It was hard for Oz to imagine what it would be like without him on board.

The pilot observed Sergeant Young approaching from across the courtyard. "What's the score?" Oz asked as the man drew near.

"We're down to four men, including myself, sir," Sergeant Young reported gloomily. "We have our medic, a machine gunner, and a rifleman. The rest of 'em were chewed up in the attack."

Oz shook his head. "Let's try to sleep," he said, glancing at his watch. "It's six hours until sunrise. You four board the chopper and sleep in there. I'll take the first watch."

Talam shivered in the chill of what remained of the night. "How much farther do we have to go?" he asked his father.

"Not far," Qaim answered, throwing his heavy saddle over the back of the kneeling dromedary. "We should reach the hideout by noon, with any luck, then our job will be completed."

They saddled their protesting animals and loaded the supplies onto the pack camels. After the prince was secured to his saddle and the other riders mounted, the beasts seesawed themselves to their feet, whining as they rose.

18

The young reporter looked directly into the TV camera with a coolness cultivated from hours of practicing in front of a mirror. The sound man/director cued her and the live broadcast began.

The small dish behind the cameraman beamed the camera's picture to a communications satellite in space, and from there, the signal was fed halfway around the world to a ground station located in the United States.

"Things continue to heat up here in East Sahra," Stacy Stallworth was saying, standing atop the Bhaliq Hilton, looking at the camera with an expansive view of the city behind her. "What began as a peace conference designed to bring harmony to this troubled region has developed into a disaster. Sources close to the royal family fear that the deteriorating situation will eventually lead to civil war. During the last hour, there have been unconfirmed reports that an American task force helping in the search for the missing prince was attacked last night and suffered heavy casualties."

She glanced down at her notes, then continued,

"Sources close to the monarch have disclosed that today's news conference, scheduled to take place this morning, will bring the announcement of a twenty-four hour deadline for the return of King Khadduri's son."

Stallworth looked directly into the camera as it zoomed in for a close-up. "Meanwhile, the Soviet Embassy is blaming the United States for mishandling its role in the peace conference and for failing to adequately protect the prince. With the situation deteriorating rapidly," she concluded, "the U.S. government can only hope that the prince will be found soon."

The reporter smiled at the camera, displaying her capped teeth, "For CCN, this is Stacy Stallworth in Bhaliq, East Sahra."

Oz, Death Song, and O.T. filled the MH-60K's tanks, draining the last of the fuel from the bladder the chopper had been carrying. Although the large container had been punctured several times by bullets during the fighting, the holes were all above the fuel level in the bladder.

As they struggled to complete their task, the sun assaulted them with nearly unbearable heat. By the time Oz climbed into the chopper, he was drenched in sweat despite the breeze that now blew through the open side doors and windows of the aircraft. Squinting at the bright, cloudless sky, the pilot brooded over the strange silence and blank spots in the crew's conversation now that Luger wasn't on board.

Oz had seen so many army buddies killed, he'd

refused to let himself even think about it. He decided that was how it would have to be today with Luger's injuries, knowing that worrying would accomplish nothing.

The pilot revved the engine and pulled the collective pitch lever, lifting the chopper amid a storm of sand. Within moments, he had taken the helicopter to six hundred feet. He glanced down at the fort one last time, the vermilion stains in the sand where men had bled and died erased by the distance at which the chopper flew.

Soon, the MH-60K shot above the low *erg* south of the fort; the chopper crossed vast tracts of shifting, blowing sands that engulfed nearly every other surface feature. The morning sun gave the illusion that the sand was bright white on its eastern slope and dark gray to the west.

The pilot resisted the temptation to go charging about at random in a frantic search for the missing prince. He knew the only chance for success lay in a careful, measured inspection of every inch of the desert in the pattern plotted beforehand. So he forced himself to stay calm as he resumed the grid search of the remainder of the quadrant they had covered the day before.

Death Song consulted the Doppler inertial navigation system, integrating it with the dual mission computers to give them their position. He then transferred the information to the dual cathode ray tubes by tapping the "prompt" keys along the sides of the screen. An identical display appeared on the CRT in front of the pilot.

After consulting the screen, Oz announced over

the intercom: "We're above territory we didn't cover yesterday. O.T., be sure someone is observing the area where Luger would normally be assigned."

"Mr. Jaber and Sergeant Young are on his side," O.T. replied. "Neal and Zeller are watching from my side."

The pilot glanced again at the map on his display screen. A little off course, he realized. The sand offered no reference points so it was easy to wander. He kicked the right rudder pedal to bring the helicopter onto its correct path.

The American guided the chopper forward at the near-maximum speed of 280 kilometers per hour. The *erg* eventually gave way to limestone cliffs, and a wide *hammada* valley slid past under the chopper with giddy speed; the MH-60K's shadow danced along the rocks and gravel before scurrying up the cliff, leaving the valley behind.

O.T. spoke from the gunner's compartment. "I caught a glimpse of something dark in the cut we just crossed, Captain. It might've just been shadows, but I'd like to take another look."

Oz swung the MH-60K in a tight turn that nearly put the chopper on its side, then straightened it out above the arroyo; he dropped to a lower altitude for a better view. The noise of his rotors boomed from the rock face and echoed down the narrow valley.

The black shape was half-hidden by the shadows of a cliff overlooking a dry stream.

"Better get Commander Warner," Oz ordered Death Song. The co-pilot quickly connected the onboard computers into the COMSAT relay system.

Within minutes, Warner was on the other end of the radio link.

"We'd better concentrate our air search in this area," Oz suggested to his superior, giving him their coordinates. "It might be a wild goose chase, but I can't imagine any reason Newman would have been here other than in pursuit of whoever took the prince."

"And you're sure it's Newman?" Warner queried.

"From here it looks like the corpse is burnt beyond recognition," Oz responded, studying the burnt hulk of the helicopter. "But the wreckage is definitely an MH-60K. There's no reason to think it's anyone else's, is there? Over."

"None of the countries surrounding East Sahra have similar aircraft," Warner answered. "It would almost have to be ours. Get Desert Six and Three to your position," Warner ordered. "I should tell you that you've got a deadline now. The king's announced that he'll crush whoever has kidnapped his son if the prince isn't returned within twenty-four hours."

"Then the king knows who kidnapped the prince?" Oz asked.

"I don't think so," the commander replied. "Ambassador Cookingham believes the king is going to lash out against *all* the other tribes."

"So we're looking at a full-scale civil war?"

"Exactly. It's more essential than ever that you find the prince and get him back to the peace conference at once. Over."

"I'll get the other elements of Desert Wind

here ASAP," Oz said. "Can you contact the East Sahran Military and alert them to what we've found? We could use more aircraft in our search. Over."

"Will do," Warner replied. "I do have one bit of good news for you. The NSA is realigning one of its satellites to go into orbit over northern Africa. They'll be relaying any messages of interest which they intercept. Unfortunately, we still don't have any 'Big Birds' available yet. Over."

"The NSA satellite will be better than nothing," Oz said. "So far we've been operating completely in the dark. Any help's welcome. Over."

"That's it, then. Good luck with your search. Over and out."

We'll need more than a little good luck, Oz thought to himself. After they had contacted Desert Three and Six, he took the chopper down to the crash site, creating a cyclone of dust as they landed.

Although the demolished chopper was burnt to the point that its ID numbers were illegible, the wreckage scattered across the sand was certainly an MH-60K. And the charred corpse melted into the plastic and metal interior of the cockpit was surely Newman, Oz thought as he shrouded the body with a poncho.

The captain climbed from the wrecked vehicle and spoke to the men outside. "There's nothing more we can learn here; let's spread out and see if there're any clues as to what Newman was chasing. Death Song, let's take a look over there," he pointed to the east. "When we were coming in, I thought I could see some kind of trail."

The two army airmen sloshed through the sand in the direction Oz had indicated. They soon found faint imprints in the sand.

"Tire tracks," Death Song said as they approached the double treadmarks. "These must have been made after the sandstorm; otherwise they would have been erased."

"The chances of someone driving by within just a day after the crash would be quite a coincidence," Oz said. "My bet is these were made by whoever Newman was chasing."

Death Song dropped to one knee to examine the tracks. "Looks like a jeep to me. See how wide apart the tracks are. Those faint marks are a second vehicle or maybe a small trailer that the jeep was pulling."

"I wonder how they brought him down?" Oz said.

"They might not have," the co-pilot suggested. "The tracks become fainter as they travel north; the wind must still have been blowing to cover the tracks like that. The desert storm could have caused him to crash into the cliff."

"So you think Newman was flying during the last of the storm, flew too low, and smashed into the cliff?"

Death Song nodded. "Of course they might have had a TOW or some other weapon. The kidnapping seems to have been pretty well planned. It's possible the jeep was carrying such armament."

"The conference site is toward the north. So they must be headed south."

"It would certainly appear so," Death Song

agreed, shading his eyes to peer into the distance where the tracks led.

"Let's get back to the chopper and follow the trail."

"It's too bad Desert Six and Three are so far away," Death Song said as they trudged back, following the faint tracks of the jeep.

Oz glanced at his watch. "It'll take almost an hour for them to get here."

Death Song stopped. "Look," he said, pointing to faint footprints leading to the cliff.

"Someone got out of the jeep?" Oz asked.

"Four or five people. One jumped or was thrown out—see where he landed in the sand. He got to his feet and headed this way with the others—running, judging by the space between footprints.

"And look at the faintness of the tracks; the sand must have been blowing pretty strong when they stopped." He pointed to the ground next to the rock. "They lost some water—here's where it dripped into the sand. They must have damaged their radiator in the collision."

"That might be the just break we need," Oz said, glancing up at the scorching sun. "They won't get far if the jeep's losing water. Let's follow the footprints and see where they lead."

"What've you got?" Sergeant Young inquired, jogging over to them.

"Footprints," Death Song answered, pointing to the sand. "Leading toward the cliff."

The three men pursued the imprints in the sand to within yards of the cliff and then stopped beside the mound of newly turned sand nearly engulfed by the multiple tracks.

"I hope this isn't what I think it is," Sergeant Young muttered.

"Sergeant," Oz said, "You'd better get some shovels from your field packs. We've got some digging to do."

CHAPTER

19

el-Kaukji licked his lips as he knocked at the ornate door leading to the king's suite.

The monarch himself jerked the door open. "Where's General Mahala?" King Khadduri demanded. "Didn't he get my call?"

"The general is taking part in the search," el-Kaukji answered, stepping hesitantly into the king's bedroom. The wide-eyed, mousey little man licked his lips again and tried to disregard the naked Bedouin woman frantically gathering her clothes.

"He's searching?"

"On one of the V-22s your majesty."

"By the Prophet's hairy rump," the king swore loudly as he began rampaging around the bedroom suite. "He's out playing soldier when he should be here helping *me* plan for our attack against the tribes. If he wanted to play soldier," he raged, "he should *never* have accepted the position of commander of the military forces and head of intelligence."

The king grabbed a leather-bound book from a table and hurled it across the room. "He's got too many responsibilities to be out in the field," he thundered. "I've half a mind to dismiss him and promote another general to his position."

"Yes, your majesty," the aide agreed, judging it better not to remind the monarch of the general's popularity with the military. el-Kaukji's gaze wandered back to the king's mistress, who scowled at him vengefully.

The woman had experienced the king's wrath before and resented the bad news that el-Kaukji had brought. Since she didn't intend to be there while the king vented his anger, she snatched up the last of her garments and hastily retreated through the archway leading to the bathroom.

"The kidnapping of the prince is an insult to the Tuareg tribe," the king fumed, "and our pride *demands* that this outrage be settled in blood." The monarch stopped in front of the messenger and glared at him.

el-Kaukji stood speechless, unsure what response the king might be wanting from him.

"Radio the general and tell him I *order* his return at once," the king finally said, grasping a hand mirror from a table and stroking his beard as he contemplated his image.

"Yes, your highness," the aide answered, clearing his throat. He bowed deeply as he prepared to leave the chamber. As el-Kaukji closed the door behind himself, the mirror shattered against it. The color left the little man's face as he scurried to the radio room.

"This time we must succeed," Gamal Faluja instructed the four revolutionaries sitting on cushions that half encircled him in the small, whitewashed room. Each man wore a cream-colored turban and a *kumsan* tied with a dark sash. A sheathed *jambiya* nestled in the folds of each man's robe. Their clothing was so similar, each might have been a uniform.

Faluja studied the men before him. They looked pale in the bright sunlight streaming through the slit windows of the mud-brick house. "This time we must succeed," he repeated more loudly, as if trying to drum the message into their consciousness. "The Polisario Front is depending on you. When you grow faint-hearted, consider your fathers, who died trying to bring the way of the people to our land. And think of your children who will otherwise be ruled by a fat king who oppresses his people."

One of the Arabs self-consciously stared at the dirt floor. Another fretted with his belt and the third chewed at his beard. Only the fourth met Faluja's gaze.

"You look like worried sheep," Faluja chided them, fingering the mouthpiece of the *huqqah* resting in front of him. "With the prince kidnapped, our only worry is the king. If we assassinate him, it will be simple to install our party during the confusion. I need not remind you, four of the generals have agreed to help us and half the army will be behind us if we succeed."

He lifted the mouthpiece of the water pipe to his lips and drew through its tube.

"But our failure with the car bomb," one of the men protested. "So many dead and maimed."

"And now the king *understands* someone wants to kill him," the bearded man added.

Faluja smiled broadly and blew a perfect smoke ring into the air. "Pain and travail are part of every birth," he said softly; "and so it is with the birth of a nation. In the end it is worth it, but countries *are born* in blood."

"What about the Americans soldiers?" the bearded man interjected.

"The king foolishly limited their numbers," Faluja answered. "And our Libyan friends shot down over half their aircraft before they even reached Bhaliq. They are, as our Chinese partners have said, a 'paper tiger'. There is nothing to fear from them." He puffed luxuriantly from his *huqqah,* then declared quietly, "This time, I will perform the task myself."

The four were silent, their surprise clearly written on their faces.

"You must be ready when I succeed to help me escape."

"We will help you," the bearded man reassured Faluja.

Their leader puffed deeply on the pipe, then counseled, "Let us go to our homes, now. Tomorrow, the revolution will begin with the death of the tyrant."

"We can't afford to be caught on the ground if we're attacked," Oz warned, ordering O.T., Death Song, and Zeller to the helicopter.

The rest of the party encircled the shallow grave, Sergeant York and Private Neal digging rapidly with the folding spades carried in the Delta Force backpacks. They first uncovered a booted foot, confirming everyone's worst suspicions, and gradually unearthed the entire grizzly spectacle.

The corpse they finally pulled from the shallow grave was caked with dried blood, its countenance savagely mutilated beyond recognition and its fingertips severed to further discourage identification.

Private Neal swore under his breath and turned from the sight with disgust.

"Same clothes the prince was wearing," Oz said, kneeling down by the remains.

"You figure they brought the prince clear out here in the middle of nowhere to snuff him?" Sergeant Young asked. "That doesn't make sense, does it?"

"It would if they wanted to keep the prince's death a secret," Oz submitted. "More than one kidnapper has killed the victim and still demanded and received a ransom."

"That's true," the sergeant nodded.

"Private Neal," Oz said, noting the soldier's pallor. "Get a poncho from the chopper and let's see if we can keep these flies off the body."

"Yes, sir," Neal answered, turning and hastily departing for the MH-60K.

"Many of the tribesmen at the peace conference wore this type of clothing," Mahmoud Jaber interjected, kneeling beside the bloody corpse. "This may not be the prince at all. Look, he has a single ring on what's left of his right hand."

"If I remember correctly," Oz said, studying the ring on the stubbed finger, "Prince Sulaiman wore two rings on that hand."

"Maybe whoever did this stole one of them," Sergeant Young suggested.

"But I don't think he was wearing a ruby ring," Oz said. "This one isn't like either of the rings he wore."

"No," Jaber agreed. "He wore a sapphire ring and another with the royal crest."

"That's what I remember, too."

"They wouldn't steal those rings and substitute this one, would they?" Sergeant Young suggested.

"If they were trying to conceal his identity they would," Jaber conceded.

"So we've come full circle," Oz said disgustedly.

"Captain!" Zeller yelled, sprinting toward the group. "We've got company."

Oz looked in the direction Zeller was pointing. Coming in low over the arroyo was a formation of planes.

CHAPTER

20

"We're almost there," Qaim announced to his sons. And none too soon, he added to himself. They'd almost exhausted their water, and the sun was becoming unbearable on the playa.

"Allah be praised," Talam muttered happily through blistered lips.

Qaim smiled to himself at his son's devoutness. As far as Qaim was concerned, Islamic disciplines suited Arabs as long as they remained impoverished. The religion offered fasting for the hungry, pilgrimage for the nomad, absolution to the waterless, and almsgiving for the pauper. With the pay I'll receive for this job, I'll be able to completely forget such dogma, the assassin assured himself.

The playa they approached was a dry lake bed carved over the centuries by the rarely-flowing streams from the nearby hills and mountain. The years of runoff and rapid evaporation had left a massive buildup of salt and alkaline. Now the winds whipped the chemicals into the air, stinging the eyes and burning the lungs.

It was worse even than the *khamsin,* the assassin

reflected, the oppressive winds that blew from the Sahara during the hottest part of spring and early summer.

His thoughts returned to his sons. "I know that this has been difficult for you," the assassin said as they bounced along on their tired dromedaries. "And I suspect you have had to do many things you find abhorrent. You will grow used to it with time. And our client will make it worthwhile for us." The younger men maintained a respectful silence.

"You must learn to abandon many of the old ways," he continued. "We are still Bedouins, still a family. Your time of hardship is almost at an end and you will have enabled our family to prevail."

Still no one spoke. Their attention was focused now on the band of horsemen that had appeared from behind a nearby hill, charging toward the small caravan at breakneck speed and churning up a white alkaline cloud as they came.

As the incoming aircraft drew nearer, the American troops sprinted for the helicopter. Oz scrambled into the steaming interior of the chopper and glanced toward Death Song.

"It's okay, captain," the co-pilot reassured him. "They're East Sahran Military."

"Boy, that's a relief!" Oz said, taking a deep breath and sighing.

"I don't know how they got here so fast," Death Song remarked.

The five V-22s rotated their twin rotors and settled onto the desert floor a short way from the helicopter, raising a storm of dust.

Oz darted from his chopper and trudged through the sand toward the three soldiers that had climbed out of the nearest airplane. "General Mahala," the pilot said, recognizing the officer's scarred face.

"Captain," the soldier acknowledged. "We received word that you had found wreckage. We were in the area and came directly to your location."

"I'm afraid we found more than just debris from the crash, general. We also uncovered a body."

"Your army pilot, of course," the general said.

"Well, yes, sir. But a second corpse was buried in the sand. There's the possibility that it could be the prince."

"The prince!" Mahala cried. He turned and gave an order in Arabic to one of the officers next to him. The soldier hastened off to the nearest V-22.

"If you Americans have allowed the prince to get killed," the general began, looking daggers at Oz.

Mahala didn't complete his threat. The American pilot said nothing.

"Where's the body?" the Bedouin demanded. He was livid, and his hands shook uncontrollably.

"This way," Oz said evenly, and led the two Arabs to the form that lay in the shadow of the cliff.

"I told the king bringing you Americans in was a mistake," Mahala muttered under his breath as the small knot of men crossed the sand.

Oz made no answer.

When they reached the corpse, the general stood silently for a few seconds, then motioned his aide to uncover the body. The East Sahran soldier bent down, pulled the poncho away, and unexpectedly emitted a hoarse cry of dismay.

Mahala stared at the body. Then he knelt beside it and jerked back the left shirtsleeve of the corpse, turning its stiff forearm from side to side. Satisfied with his inspection, he stood, clapping the sand off his hands. "You can cover the remains," he said and turned back to Oz. "And *you* can thank your lucky stars this isn't Prince Sulaiman."

"You're certain?"

"Of course I'm certain!" Mahala exploded. "The prince has a birthmark on his left forearm. Whoever this was had no such mark."

Oz spoke up, "General, we found tire—"

"Just stay out of this," the Bedouin angrily interrupted Oz. "My men will take care of this corpse and the one in your wrecked helicopter. Just get away from here."

"But there's something you should know," Oz said irritably.

"Please spare me, Captain," Mahala hissed. "We have the manpower to conduct a *real* air search; how you thought you could do anything with just three choppers is beyond me. You Americans are so arrogant. We were fools to let you try to help us."

He turned and stormed away, his aide following along behind.

Sergeant Young expertly spit chewing tobacco on one of the many flies buzzing the corpse. "Guess you don't need to tell him about the tire tracks since he already knows it all. Right, captain?"

Oz didn't answer. "Let's get to the chopper," he said.

＊　　＊　　＊

Gamal Faluja watched through the rifle scope as the king stood behind the platform that had been erected for the outdoor press conference. The cameras were in place and the press corp mulled around, unable to observe the monarch standing behind the large curtain.

"My son? Dead?" King Khadduri asked the messenger incredulously.

"That's all we have, your highness," el-Kaukji replied. "General Mahala's aide called to report that a body had been found and that it was believed to be your son."

The king was stunned. "Take me to the palace," he ordered his bodyguards.

"What of the news conference, your majesty?" el-Kaukji implored.

"To hell with them. My son is dead. Tell them that: my son is dead."

el-Kaukji bowed deeply as the king trudged slowly back toward his waiting limousine.

Realizing that something had gone wrong and that he was fast losing his chance to assassinate the king, Gamal Faluja frantically aligned the crosshairs of his rifle on the monarch's head as the man approached his car.

21

Oz briskly accelerated, lifting the chopper to one thousand feet to remain on East Sahra radar, then heading northward, away from the crash site.

When he had traveled six kilometers, the pilot warned his crew and passengers, "Everyone hang on; we're going to get lost." With that, he dropped the aircraft into a steep dive.

The occupants of the helicopter seemed to hang in their seatbelts as they started a near free-fall descent toward the plain far below. Oz expertly brought them out of the dive, leveling off when he was low enough to be lost by radar in the ground clutter.

Once the pilot was certain he could no longer be detected, he turned southward and switched to TF/TA, skimming along the surface of the desert parallel to the arroyo where they'd seen the jeep's tire tracks.

When they had passed the V-22s resting in the dry stream bed, the pilot lifted the chopper over the edge of the cliff and dropped into the narrow valley.

"There're so many people walking around at

the crash sight," Death Song remarked, "I suspect the tire tracks will be obliterated soon."

"We'll tell General Mahala what we've found after he cools off," Oz said. "But in the meantime, let's see if the tracks lead anywhere. I'd sure like to be the first one to find the prince, considering I lost him."

"There's the trail!" Death Song exclaimed. "I can barely make out the tracks."

"I see it," Oz confirmed. "Now let's see where it leads."

Gamal Faluja kept his face tight against the cheek rest of the rifle stock as he centered the scope on the king's skull. The gunman's finger eased against the weapons's sensitive trigger.

The king stepped aside to speak briefly to the driver, putting a bodyguard between the would-be assassin and his prey.

Faluja waited patiently.

The ruler appeared again. The gunman centered the scope, his finger caressing the trigger.

The king was nearly in the car, his head bobbing. Faluja knew better than to hurry the shot, and lowered the Fusil Modèle 1 sniper rifle. The adage that you must kill a king quickly if at all came to the gunman's mind.

He knew he was right to wait, although the frustration welling up inside him was overpowering. To come so close, he lamented.

But when he did shoot Khadduri, it would be quick and final. A lingering death could send the country into a protracted civil war.

The revolutionary watched the limousine far below him speed away, leaving the press still awaiting the monarch's appearance. Faluja wondered what had caused the sovereign to leave so abruptly, especially since Khadduri was trying to generate public support for his genocidal war against the country's minorities.

"I hope they haven't rescued his son," Faluja thought, folding the integral bipod of his rifle and cycling the bolt eight times to eject the cartridges from the chamber and magazine of the bolt-action gun. He carefully replaced the firearm into the delivery package he'd carried into the building with him.

The would-be assassin stood and adjusted his jump suit, its insignia proclaiming, in English and Arabic, the falsehood that he was an employee of the Bhaliq phone company. The suit that had cost him such a tiny sum afforded him entry wherever he pleased.

Abd el Taha Izaak sat on a boulder watching the cloudless sky, wondering if the travelers had said the truth.

It was hard for the old man to imagine why the Americans would be interested in the desert area where the Qahidi tribe lived. The land barely supported the tribe's few animals. The Bedouin inspected the sparse grass growing at the base of the cliffs and reached over to pat the black goat nibbling at the dry plants.

Were the Americans going to start herding goats and sheep? he smiled to himself.

He shooed a fly that had lit on his knee.

Perhaps it is our well they need, Izaak reflected more seriously. The tribesman could comprehend fighting for water—any Bedouin could understand that. He scratched his head, trying to puzzle out an answer.

Of course the story about the Americans might be a lie, he realized.

Certainly the travelers were not trustworthy—he'd realized that when he'd inspected the jeep and noted the tiny water leak in its radiator. He knew no vehicle could run for long in the desert without water, and there was none of the precious liquid to waste on a leaking radiator.

But if any tricks had been played in the trade, he smiled, they were his. His son knew how to disassemble and repair the radiator using a campfire to heat a metal soldering iron; so they would have the jeep repaired in no time.

On the other hand, one of the dromedaries he'd traded had a bad leg. There was little doubt it would go lame—in months if not weeks. Then the desert travelers would regret having tried to trick Izaak. The patriarch smiled hugely to himself.

A Qahidi tribesman, his robes flapping in the desert breeze, approached the old man. Izaak recognized the Bedouin even though his face was veiled against the dust. There was no doubt that the worried brow belonged to Gamasy.

"Our half-track is hidden," Gamasy told his *qa'id.*

"And the rockets and machine guns?" Izaak queried.

"As you instructed us," Gamasy replied. "The

young men who have learned to use them are herding their goats nearby. We can bring the weapons into action within moments of sighting the Americans.''

"And they have been cautioned to wait for my signal?" Izaak asked. He didn't want an overzealous Qahidi youth to shoot at an East Sahran military plane by mistake.

"Yes, they have been forewarned."

Izaak deliberated for a moment to be sure he hadn't missed anything. It had been a long time since the Qahidi had actually engaged in a battle. Many had never fired a shot in anger, and it was Izaak's responsibility as *qa'id* to think everything through.

The women had been instructed to hide in the cave by their tents. The older tribesmen were armed, and the younger men, trained for the approaching civil war, manned the modern weapons that had been supplied to the tribe. Everything seemed in order.

Izaak noted the other man's fidgeting; the *qa'id* smiled and nodded. "You have done well," he told his companion as he stood up. "If the Americans come looking for trouble, they will get more than they bargained for."

The MH-60K skimmed the arroyo floor. Inside the chopper, the heat was nearly unbearable. Oz lifted the visor on his helmet, pushing the sweat away from his eyes. The APQ-168 terrain following/terrain avoidance radar automatically hauled the MH-60K helicopter into a tight climb over a dune that had invaded the dry stream bed. The tire tracks also turned away from the arroyo, prompting Oz to push against a pedal and point the chopper in the appropriate direction.

The MH-60K leaped the wall of the cliff, creating a G-force that pushed the chopper's occupants into their seats, then flung them upward. As they cleared the edge of the rise, the TF/TA radar vectored them downward in a giddy dive.

They continued following the tracks which led over a *barchan* dune. As the chopper lifted over the sandy rise, Oz abruptly found himself hurtling toward a cluster of tents at the base of a stretch of rocky hills.

"So much for surprise, if that's where the jeep was headed," Oz muttered over the intercom.

If the encampment ahead was the vehicle's destination, Oz realized they could expect an attack from the ground. "Arm our weapons," he ordered his co-pilot.

Death Song flipped the switches. "Weapons armed," he announced.

As the Americans overflew the camp, a young Qahidi tribesmen concealed behind a hill readied his Euromissile "HOT" rocket launcher, waiting for the helicopter to get within range. Hearing the chopper's approach, the young warrior aligned the tripod-mounted weapon on its target, acquired the helicopter in his sights, and pulled against the launch trigger.

22

"Rocket launch!" O.T. warned the pilot from his position in the gunner's window.

Oz immediately threw the chopper into a short dive, skimming along the sand to prevent the missile from having more than one chance to strike. Death Song activated the counter-measures pod, and a stream of chaff erupted from the system, tumbling over the surface of the earth.

The metallic flakes of chaff were lost in the dust churned up by the passage of the rotor blades as the missile remained locked onto the aircraft.

Oz jerked the control column to the side and kicked a rudder pedal, turning the nose of the chopper to the right. Then he promptly forced the MH-60K to the left, hoping to fake out the missile's controller, although the pilot didn't know for certain that the oncoming projectile was being guided.

A .50-caliber machine gun fired on the chopper as it turned. The ground fire cut into the cabin, pocking the windscreen in front of the pilot, who continued the tight turn.

A fraction of a second later, the missile flashed by the aircraft.

The projectile exploded in the sand far ahead of the chopper, sending a plume of fire and dust into the air. The machine gun below the chopper lost its target, leaving the metal detector warning lights on the console and the holes stitched in the windscreen to remind the pilot of the ground attack.

"I'm going to put some sand between us and the camp," Oz said, guiding his helicopter over a dune and dropping behind it.

Even though the chopper was no longer visible from the camp, another concealed machine gun took aim at the Americans. The weapon sent a stream of tracers slicing through the air over the cockpit, dropping toward the chopper targeting the camouflaged machine gun nest.

Oz thumbed the fire button on the control column. The twin guns in the pod to the right of the chopper rattled, dropping the empty casings as the aircraft hurtled toward its target.

The .30-caliber Lewis gun on the ground had little effect on the MH-60K. The same could not be said of the bullets smashing into the machine gun nest. The projectiles ripped into the drum magazine atop the weapon, tearing it apart and spraying the gunner with shell fragments. The gun jammed on the broken magazine as the chopper thundered over the position.

"Should we contact the East Sahran Military?" Death Song inquired.

Oz thought for a moment, then replied, "We can't afford to wait 'til they get here because the kidnappers might kill the prince by then. We're going to have to give them everything we've got right now."

"Desert Six and Three?" the co-pilot asked.

"That's a good idea. Get me onto their frequency."

The pilot triggered on his radio. "Desert One calling Six, come in please. Over."

"This is Desert Six reading you loud and clear, One."

"We've located the campsite where we believe the prince is being held." The pilot quickly read the coordinates to the AH-64 pilot. "We're taking fire and are going to initiate our own counterattack. If you don't hear from us shortly, contact the East Sahrans. Got that? Over."

"Roger, One. Our ETA to your area is forty minutes. You sure you don't want to wait for us?"

"That's a negative, Six, but thanks for the offer. Desert One signing off, over and out."

The pilot skimmed another hill, dropping toward the ground to put the dune between him and the attackers. "Sergeant Young," he called over the intercom.

"Yes, sir?" the soldier answered over the headset he wore.

"Let's set you and your men down and see if you can take on some of these guys," the pilot suggested. "After we drop you off, we'll circle and come in from the south."

"Sounds good to me," Young answered. He signaled to Zeller, Neal, and his machine gunner.

Within seconds, the four Delta Force troopers

had freed themselves from their seat harnesses, grabbed their weapons, and leaped into the hot sand as the chopper bounced on its hydraulic landing struts with the speed of their decent.

Sergeant Young flashed a thumbs-up sign and waved at the chopper.

"They're clear," O.T. called from the gunner's compartment behind Oz.

Oz lifted the chopper into the air, creating a squall of sand and dust. He stayed close to the ground, circling southward for an attack run at the Qahidi camp.

"Desert One," the radio crackled as Oz rounded the camp. "This is Ground One," Young called. "We're in place. The guys in the nest you hit are no problem; one's high-tailing it to the camp, but I don't think he saw us. We'll wait here until he clears the dune and then push on toward the next machine gun emplacement when you head in. Over."

"Good," Oz called back. "I'll be in position in about thirty seconds to make a run from the south. Over."

"That's a roger. Over and out."

The pilot shoved the control column forward for greater speed. The aircraft narrowly missed the rocky ledge ahead of them, its fixed wheels racing past the limestone outcropping with only inches of clearance.

"Machine gun nest at two o'clock," Death Song announced, pointing out the window.

"Got it," Oz said. "They've got their campsite pretty well covered." He altered the chopper's

course and tapped the red button on the control column to send a single folding-fin, 2.75-inch rocket
from its 12-pack pod. The missile hissed out of its
tube, racing toward the machine gun, and striking
just ahead of the emplacement.

A shower of sand bowled the MAS 52 machine
gun off its tripod. The Bedouins, who now posed no
immediate threat to the Americans, scrambled for
cover as the helicopter screamed overhead.

"We're at the top of the hill overlooking another position," Young called on the radio. "We
haven't been seen. We're going in now."

Oz watched the terrain ahead of him, shoving
down on the collective pitch lever so the MH-60K
dropped to follow the rolling hill ahead of them.
"Okay, Ground One, we're about there, so all hell's
going to break loose in a second," Oz warned.
"Whenever possible, take out the weapons and spare
the personnel; we don't want to create an interna-
tional incident. Over."

"Roger that," Young returned.

The helicopter topped the final hill and the Bedouin camp, spreading out before it, erupted in gunfire of all types.

Most of the weapons were old bolt-action rifles,
several were G3 military rifles, and a cloud of blue
smoke marked the position of a tribesman firing an
ancient muzzle loader. Oz ignored the hail of small-
arms fire pattering against the armored skin of the
chopper and concentrated on the half-track that appeared in front of them, the machine gun in its turret
blazing.

The pilot slowed his chopper, kicking a pedal

to align it with the vehicle, and launched two rockets from their tubes.

Oz immediately pushed the chopper forward. It accelerated over the armored vehicle as the rockets found their targets, ripping the track off its rear and half-tearing the turret apart, throwing the gunner into the sand.

O.T. punched a ten-shot string of fire from his GE M134 Minigun. The six-barreled muzzles blurred as the Gatling-like weapon sent another fusillade earthward, ripping into an APC lumbering out of its camouflage netting. The Minigun fired, automatically yanking ammunition from its four-thousand round linked belt and shoving the cartridges into the six revolving bolts as it spit out the empties.

The pilot rotated his fighting machine above the encampment, his machine guns blazing and rockets streaking. He fired quickly, but carefully avoided all areas where he thought the prince might be or where innocent women and children could be hidden. "Where do you suppose they'd have the prince?" Oz called above the din.

"How about that big tent in the center of the camp?" O.T. yelled back.

Oz shoved the helicopter toward the main structure, coming in low so the front wheels of the chopper snagged into the fabric of the tent. He yanked hard on the collective pitch lever, taking the chopper almost straight up.

He'd hoped to rip the tent apart.

Instead, the animal-skin structure wrapped around the landing gear of the chopper and pulled the machine earthward. Then the powerful rotors of the MH-60K pulled it upward, lifting the whole structure with it and ripping it from its poles and tent pegs.

As the tent followed the freed chopper, flapping in the wash from the rotors, the down-draft suddenly tore it free of the wheels, and it floated downward like a giant black parachute. Several of the men on the ground ran frantically to escape the falling tent but were engulfed under its folds when it reached the earth.

Oz swung the helicopter past the encampment and prepared for another attack, unaware of the hand-held missiles being leveled at him.

Sergeant Young cautiously approached the machine gun nest, his desert camouflage uniform blending into the terrain. The gunners manning the emplacement stood peering at the helicopter in the camp below, their backs toward the Delta Force troopers stealing up the hill.

Young and Zeller jumped the sandbags surrounding the emplacement. Young cold-cocked the Bedouin closest to him with the barrel of his Colt carbine, striking at the base of the man's skull. Zeller used the stock of his weapon to hit the gunner's spine between his shoulder blades.

Young signaled the other two troopers toward the position, then concentrated on trussing the unconscious Bedouins with the plastic ties he carried for such purposes.

"Think you can take out that missile launcher

over there with your handy-dandy sniper rifle?"
Young asked Zeller, pointing toward the rocket.

"Missile?" the Oklahoman asked, squinting into
the sun.

"There to the east. On that V-shaped rise."

"Oh sure," Zeller replied, spotting it. He carefully rested his rifle on the sandbag, lying on his belly
so the firearm would be as steady as possible. He
peered through the Unertl scope that now replaced
the night-vision scope on the Insight Systems receiver assembly. The details of the missile tube came
into sharp focus in the quality optics of the scope.

The rifleman tapped the set trigger and the gun
thundered, adding to the din drifting up from the
camp. The 62-grain bullet found its mark, hitting the
optical aiming system of the rocket launcher and
shattering its innards. Fragments of glass and plastic
peppered the man holding the launcher, inducing
him to drop it and run.

"Nice shooting," Young said. "Now, see that
guy over there dragging that other launcher into
place?"

Zeller glanced in the direction the sergeant was
pointing. "Piece of cake," he smiled.

Abd el Taha Izaak, the leader of the Qahidi, was
amazed at how rapidly the chopper had wrecked his
settlement. What he couldn't understand was why
none of his rocket launchers had come into play
against the Americans. Izaak cursed the day he had
been born *qa'id*.

"There is an American up there," Gamasy

alerted his leader, pointing toward the machine gun emplacement overlooking the camp.

"That's *our* man," Izaak admonished Gamasy. "What are you—"

He stopped in mid-sentence at the sight of the curved helmet barely visible over the top of the sand bags. Izaak muttered a curse that was old when Mohammed was born.

So the Americans are on the ground, too, Izaak thought bitterly. How poorly he had planned. He longed for the days when men fought with scimitars on the backs of horses or camels.

You must fight for today, not the past, he told himself as he shouldered his weapons. Before he could squeeze off a shot, he saw a rifle muzzle flash from the machine gun nest.

Izaak's shoulder felt like a camel had kicked it.

He dropped his rifle, falling to his knees and grasping the bloody hole that had appeared in his shoulder. He rolled behind a boulder as a second bullet cracked over his head. "Get down!" he warned Gamasy who stood dumb-founded at the unexpected attack.

The other Bedouin stumbled in behind the boulder. "Does it hurt?" Gamasy asked solicitously.

"Of course it hurts, you fool!" Izaak bellowed. "Tie a white rag to my rifle."

"We are surrendering?"

"No," Izaak hissed, listening to the helicopter circle the camp, for another attack. "We will fight to the death if necessary. But perhaps we can parley with them. An honorable settlement would be preferable to being killed for no apparent reason."

Gamasy nodded, taking the rifle from his *qa'id*.

CHAPTER

23

King Khadduri was in a state of shock.

First his son had been reported dead, and then, within fifteen minutes, General Mahala had radioed that the body was someone else. Mahala had been ordered back to the palace immediately, and the monarch, in a fit of rage, had proceeded to trash the dining hall where he'd received the news.

The palace servants knew to stay discreetly hidden during the king's rampage. When another messenger arrived, the cursing and glass-breaking stopped abruptly. Only then did the staff venture into the dining hall to clean up the mess, knowing that the room would be needed in three hours for the next meal—which King Khadduri always demanded be served at its regular hour. The servants knew at least one entire staff that had become beggars because they'd failed to have the monarch's meal ready on time.

Moments later, el-Kaukji, the king's aide, knocked at King Khadduri's office door where the monarch had sequestered himself.

"Go away!"

"It is very important, my sovereign."

"It had better be," King Khadduri declared grumpily, recognizing the voice of his aide. "Enter."

el-Kaukji cautiously peered into the room, then stepped inside after ascertaining that his emir wasn't preparing to throw anything. "Your highness, you have a visitor."

"I wish to see no one," the king stated, staring intently at a bound volume of Arabic poetry.

el-Kaukji swallowed hard and spoke again. "It is Saima."

The king glanced up from his book. "Send him in at once. And then leave us alone."

el-Kaukji escorted Saima into the king's office, then quietly stole away, securing the massive door behind himself.

"Your highness," Saima bowed.

"Why wasn't I warned about the bomb attack?" King Khadduri demanded, slamming his book down on the desktop in front of him. "There's no use having a spy if you can't warn me of such things beforehand!"

Saima decided not to tell the potentate that he had also nearly let him be shot as well. Instead, Saima said, "Faluja is careful. He doesn't let us leave his sight for even a few minutes. Even then, he often pairs us so one of the others is watching. It was impossible for me to phone or get away until now. I'm only here because Faluja thinks I'm on an errand for him. Here is the name of the man who is responsible for the car bomb."

The potentate took the slip of paper. "Good. Now when will he try to kill me again?"

"Tomorrow during the press conference."

"How will it be done?"

Saima paused a moment, trying to arrange his thoughts so he wouldn't betray the fact that he'd nearly let Faluja kill the ruler prior to the earlier scheduled press conference. The informant was positive the sovereign wouldn't understand that Saima didn't want to risk certain death to save the monarch's life. Finally he spoke, "Faluja has a scoped rifle. He is planning to kill you himself by firing from atop the building overlooking the press stage. The general he is working for will then take over immediately."

"Do you have the general's name?" the potentate queried.

"No, your highness. Faluja still has not told us their names."

King Khadduri tapped the desktop a moment. "I'll have my secret police ready to apprehend Faluja and his men before the press conference tomorrow." The ruler leaned back into his chair and looked directly at Saima. "You did one thing right, anyway. Faluja did relay the information you fed him about the American convoy to the Libyans; their attack was better than we had any right to expect."

The king toyed with a crystal paperweight. "Do you think he'd buy your story again if you gave him the whereabouts of the Americans?"

Saima worried the idea over, weighing the dangers to himself. "I'm not sure, your majesty."

"I would double your pay," the king proposed. "Those Americans are close to finding the prince."

"Triple it and I would be willing to risk it."

"Double, or I'll make a call to Faluja and see what he thinks of your treachery," the potentate warned.

"I'm sure double would be fine," Saima said, bowing.

"We have received word from the Americans again. It seems they attacked a Qahidi camp, thinking the prince was being held there." The king smiled as he thought of the Americans assaulting his enemies. "So we know their approximate whereabouts. Here are the coordinates."

Saima took the paper and hid it in the folds of his soiled *kumsan.*

"See if Faluja can get the coordinates to the Libyans immediately," the king directed. "I'm not sure how fast the Libyans can scramble their aircraft, but the Americans will probably be in the area for only a short time."

Saima bowed.

"And get the name of the general," the monarch demanded. "Keep your ears open."

"Yes, your majesty."

"Then go!" the king ordered. "Faluja will be wondering what is taking you so long."

"It's important to let the Bedouins save face," Mahmoud Jaber informed Oz over the intercom.

"I'll keep that in mind," Oz said to the Arab translator. "In the meantime, how do I know this truce flag isn't a trap?"

"You don't," Jaber smiled. "But I trust Izaak; I can't imagine him breaking a truce."

Oz refrained from mentioning that the last time he'd staked anything on tribal taboos, he'd managed to get drugged and lose the prince. Instead, he triggered the radio, "Ground One, this is Desert One, come in."

"Read you loud and clear, Desert One," Sergeant Young answered.

"I'm taking the chopper in to meet the guy with the white flag. How's it look from down there?"

"The Bedouin with the flag seems to have ordered everyone to stop shooting. And Zeller has pretty well knocked out all their missile launchers with his sniper rifle."

"Good," Oz said. "Keep a sharp lookout on the hills while we go in. We'll keep track of things around the chopper."

"Will do," Sergeant Young said.

Oz circled the camp, searching for any sign of an ambush, before setting the chopper down in the center of the Qahidi camp.

Mahmoud Jaber instructed the Americans to stay on the helicopter, then stepped out of the MH-60K, pushing his way through the crowd of Bedouins that surrounded the chopper, and embraced Abd el Taha Izaak.

"It has been a long time," Jaber told his old friend.

"Too long," Izaak admitted. "And to meet under such circumstances. Tell me what is going on."

Jaber rapidly described the events at the peace

conference and told how the Americans were searching for the men who had driven the jeep to the
Qahidi camp.

"By Allah, I knew those men weren't to be
trusted," Izaak said after hearing the story. "We
traded for the jeep and, I'm afraid, believed their
story. They said the Americans were apt to attack
us," Izaak explained. "So when you passed over, one
of my men fired his rocket without permission." The
old tribesman shook his head. "After that, you answered in kind and we were committed to the battle.
Will the Americans ever believe us?"

"I'm sure they will," Jaber answered. "We must
get one of their medics to tend to your wounds—and
to those of your people. These Americans can be a
pain in the bowels. But they also can be helpful."

"You must smooth things over between us,
then," Izaak instructed the translator.

Jaber climbed back aboard the helicopter and
explained to Oz what the Bedouin *qa'id* had related
to him.

"Do you think he's telling the truth?" Oz asked.

"I do," Jaber replied. "Izaak is an old friend."

"Then all this fighting . . ." Oz began.

"Was an honest mistake," Jaber finished. "I'd
suggest that if your medic were to help the wounded,
it would go a long way toward promoting peace."

Within minutes, Private Neal was tending to
the *qa'id*'s shoulder wound.

"Tell him he's lucky," the medic told Jaber,
checking the bandage to make sure it was secure.
"The bullet made quite a hole but it didn't break any

bones or hit a lung. He'll probably always have a stiff shoulder but it will heal in a few weeks."

"I can't believe no one was killed," O.T. confided to Oz, glancing at one of the wounded.

"It's lucky Zeller was aiming for hardware rather than humans," Sergeant Young added, jamming a wad of tobacco into his mouth.

"Captain," Death Song called over the radio.

Oz removed his portable radio from its pouch. "Roger."

"We've got Desert Six and Desert Three headed our way. ETA in three minutes."

"Good. Tell the medic on Three to be ready to get to work. We have a lot of wounded Bedouins still needing attention."

"Will do."

Oz put away his radio and walked over to Izaak and Jaber. "Please convey my apologies to the *qa'id,*" he directed Jaber. "I'm very sorry we attacked his village. Tell him that when we saw the rocket launched at us—and the jeep tracks leading here—we assumed the villagers were involved in the kidnapping of Prince Sulaiman."

Jaber spoke to Izaak who replied in Arabic, punctuating his remarks with rapid hand gestures.

The translator turned back to Oz. "He says that the men who sold him the jeep had one prisoner with them. An older man and three younger held him, each was armed with a rifle."

"Has Izaak ever seen Prince Sulaiman?" the pilot asked.

Jaber relayed the American's question to the

Bedouin *qa'id*. "He says he has not," Jaber translated.

"Have him describe the bound man," the pilot directed. "Let's see if the descriptions match."

After a brief discussion, Jaber turned back to Oz. "He's certain that Prince Sulaiman was with them. The stranger was the right height, wore the same clothing, and had on the rings we thought the prince was wearing the night of the banquet."

Izaak spoke again to Jaber.

"The *qa'id* asks that you stay and banquet with his tribe," Jaber translated for Oz. "He desires to make amends."

"Tell him we'd be honored, but first we must find the prince. As to amends, tell him we were as much at fault as he was. Convey our apologies and assure him we will return after we find the prince."

The *qa'id* began speaking rapidly and gesturing.

Jaber translated: "Izaak asks that he and his best warriors be allowed to accompany you on your search for the prince. He feels he has a score to settle with the men who tricked him into attacking you. This is a matter of importance to him," Jaber explained. "The tribe's pride has been violated by these men. The Qahidi live by a moral code that demands retribution for an insult to their tribal pride. Izaak says that he surmises your helicopter can haul more than four soldiers. And he wants you to know that the men he will send are highly skilled in fighting and in the ways of the desert."

Twenty-three thousand, six hundred miles above the earth over northern Africa, the retro jets of the KH-25 man-made moon stabilized it into a new orbit. While the satellite didn't come to rest in a perfectly geosynchronous orbit, its drift would keep it in place for several weeks—long enough to accomplish its assigned task.

The signal intelligence, or SIGINT, satellite extended its antennae and sat in the silence of space, eavesdropping on the magnetic frequencies scattered throughout the atmosphere below it. It processed the babel of signals to remove commercial broadcasts and electrical noise. Then it relayed the purified signals to a second geosynchronous satellite a quarter of the way around the world to then be bounced earthward to a twenty-foot dish antenna atop the National Security Agency's headquarters at Fort George G. Meade in Maryland.

Because processing the vast number of intercepts was beyond anything human beings were capable of, the organizing and filtering of the messages was handled by complex computers at the NSA, many of which enjoyed an artificial intelligence capable of weighing the importance of the communiques.

The computers searched for any mention of Prince Sulaiman's whereabouts and for an increase in the pattern and volume of signals normally associated with plans for initiating battle—in this case an East Sahran civil war. With infinite patience and incredible speed, the machines conducted their search with quiet efficiency, transferring their findings of what was happening in East Sahra to the chief of communications.

As the human being in the chain of events and the communications chief for the KH-25, Tania

Trevino had the final responsibility for conveying the information to CIA headquarters and the Pentagon.

She was good at her job.

Those who worked with the prim forty-year-old found Trevino cold, and easily understood her affinity for emotionless computers. But no one at the NSA would suggest that she didn't do her job well. When it came to evaluating what the electronic devices under her command had uncovered, she had no equals.

As the messages from Northern Africa dropped from the sky, Trevino worked at a terminal with access to the machines. She carefully adjusted the electronic brains' algorithms to lock onto the information she sought.

Data had been entering the complex for only a few minutes when the first "hit" sounded and the computers signaled the chief of communications.

"There must be some malfunction," the computer operator told Trevino.

She ignored him and studied the decoded message that had been coughed onto the screen for her inspection. Then she lifted the red phone on her desk. After consulting a number scribbled on a note card taped to the computer monitor, she dialed the digits and waited until the phone on the other end had been picked up.

Trevino spoke quickly, "I have a flash message for Commander Warner."

She listened impatiently.

Then she spoke again, "No way, lieutenant. I said 'Flash!' That's top priority."

The voice on the other end protested.

"I don't care where he is or what he's doing," Trevino said. "Find Commander Warner at once! There's no time to lose. I'll stay on the line until you locate him."

CHAPTER

24

The twenty-two horsemen galloped across the playa, raising a white fog of choking alkaline dust. The riders wore the *keffiyeh* pulled across their faces to keep out the swirling dust. In their hands, they brandished swords and SAR 80 rifles.

Talam lifted his Mauser.

"No," Qaim warned him. "Put away the weapon and let me handle this."

The riders were upon the caravan within minutes. To surround the prince and his escort, the horsemen broke into two columns, their steeds' hooves thumping upon the dry earth.

The leader of the horsemen pulled down his *keffiyeh,* exposing his weathered face.

Qaim did likewise.

"You have done well," the leader said. "We have your hideout prepared for you. We must hurry; there have been air patrols passing over all day."

"Lead us," Qaim ordered.

The Bedouin pulled at the white stallion's reins to turn it around.

The desert horsemen led Qaim, his sons, and

the prince deeper into the playa. The alkaline-impregnated earth slowly dropped away into smooth roadways until the men found themselves in a giant crater nearly a mile wide.

"These are old salt mines dating back at least two thousand years," a Bedouin rider next to Qaim told the assassin. "The Romans used the salt from these mines to pay their legions. Slaves from conquered nations labored and died in these mines. Later, we Bedouins traded the commodity throughout northern Africa and into the Middle East."

"I never heard of these mines," Qaim said, gazing at the pile of cut stones that were all that remained of an old Roman fort.

"They became unprofitable to operate centuries ago," the horseman explained. "But the extensive network of caves make an ideal hideout."

"Father," Parim called, kicking his dromedary to pull up alongside his father. "A *hamsin* is coming."

Qaim looked toward the south where his son was pointing. A brownish cloud of dust and sand was boiling toward them.

"Don't worry," the horseman said. "We're almost there."

"And the storm is good; it will cover our tracks," Qaim told his sons.

The Bedouin tribesmen led Qaim and his men to twin caves that gaped at the valley like the eyes of a skull. The riders continued on until they had entered the eastern cave.

Qaim found the interior of the tunnel cool and dark. A .50-caliber machine gun manned by three

Bedouins sat just inside the entrance. It took several minutes for his eyes to adjust to the dim light provided by electrical bulbs strung along the ceiling.

"During the past two years," the rider next to Qaim added, "the king has been storing supplies here, including fuel for an electrical generator to serve as his emergency hideaway. Now we've taken it over."

The horses' hooves echoed in the cave as they turned down a narrow corridor branching off the main cave, following the string of lights that led deeper into the earth. Qaim turned around in his saddle and was startled to note that the entrance to the cave was higher than they were. They were traveling down an incline into the depths of the earth.

"We're here," the horseman announced as they rounded the fork and the entrance was lost from sight. Qaim kicked his dromedary so it knelt for him to dismount.

"I think you'll find our accommodations less than spartan," the Bedouin chief told Qaim as he led the party into a large, brightly lit chamber.

Though the walls and ceiling were crudely cut from solid sheets of crystalline salt, the floor was flat and carpeted. A cluster of chairs and cushions sat in the center of the large chamber, and a tiny kitchen complete with refrigerator and microwave squatted in the corner.

"The hallway leads to a bathroom and our bedrooms," the chief gestured. "The only problem we'll have here is the corrosive action of the salt. Steel and iron rust within days. But I think you'll find your stay here quite comfortable. Now there's one little matter we must clear up," he said, drawing his long-bladed knife.

The three American choppers glided above the rolling sand dunes.

Oz stared ahead, trying to determine whether he was viewing a mirage. "Death Song, do you see movement ahead?" he finally asked his co-pilot. "Low on the horizon. I thought it was a dune, but it looks like its moving."

Death Song looked away from his instruments. "Straight ahead?"

"Yeah."

"I'm not sure. Looks like a cloud."

Oz laughed. "I hope I haven't been in the desert so long I've forgotten what clouds look like! The color looks more like sand to me."

"Hang on," Death Song said. "We've got a message coming in from our COMSAT." He glanced at the instrument panel. "The COMSAT's downloading its codes to our computer."

In a few seconds, Warner's voice came over Oz's earphones. "Desert One, we just got a priority message from the NSA. The short of it is that you've got four or five attack jets headed directly for you. Someone inside King Khadduri's government must have given them the information. Over."

"We should be able to take on five if we know they're coming in," Oz said. "We radioed our position to the East Sahran Military an hour ago and requested help in our search; they claimed they couldn't spare the aircraft."

"Real odd, considering you're trying to find the prince and avert a war," Warner interrupted.

"That *must* be where they got our coordinates," Oz said.

"I'll see if we can uncover anything else from the NSA," Warner continued. "In the meantime, you'd better get ready for the Libyans. Their ETA is between ten to twenty minutes. Do you want me to contact the East Sahran Military? Over."

"Negative on that," Oz answered. "If the East Sahrans are in on this, we don't want them to know we have an advanced warning. Plus, since they're in the dark about our tapping into their messages, we may learn more. Over."

"That's true," Warner agreed. "I should have thought of that but I'm half asleep. I'll get off the air. Good luck. Over and out."

"That cloud is a sandstorm," Oz said to Death Song, eyeing the seething mass that was engulfing the hills as it approached them. "I bet we could put that to good use before the Libyans get here."

He switched his radio on and warned Desert Six and Desert Three to expect an imminent attack from five Mirage III jets.

"Listen," Oz said to the two chopper pilots. "I think I know a way to sucker these guys. The sandstorm will provide the perfect cover."

"Won't the sand trash our engines?" asked the pilot of Desert Six.

"Not with what I have in mind," Oz replied, hastily explaining his scheme.

*   *   *

"I was this close," Gamal Faluja indicated with his thumb and index finger, "to sending the king to collect his eternal rewards." The four revolutionaries encircling him on their stained cushions listened politely. "The plan worked perfectly—except for killing the king. But since he has scheduled another press conference for tomorrow morning, we can utilize the same plan. The general who is helping our revolution will be ready, too. Since the military is apparently going onto a war footing, General Saad el-Sid will be able to strike quickly and help us take over the government."

Saad el-Sid, Saima said to himself, stroking his beard. Now he had a name to give to the king, and this whole charade could come to an end.

"And our friends in Libya have offered to aid us if we need assistance," Faluja continued, pausing to study the vacant look on Saima's face. "Did you have a question, Saima?"

"Oh, no," Saima swallowed. "I was just thinking how things would change."

"Yes, and for the better," Faluja said, warming to his favorite subject and forgetting Saima. The leader paused, a distant look coming into his eyes; Saima relaxed, thanking Allah in a silent prayer for the leader's distraction.

"The Polisario Front will succeed," the revolutionary leader almost chanted. "The ideals of Lenin were never fully put into practice in Russia, China, or the other sorry police-states that call themselves communists. East Sahra will lead the world into the future," he expostulated, pacing back and forth in the tiny mud-brick house like a professor lecturing his students.

Saima resigned himself to the long monologue about the joys of a people's republic which Faluja knew was coming. Saima blanked out the words as he always did after having learned the truth about Tienamin Square and the Khmer Rouge.

The one worthwhile thing Faluja had given Saima was the desire to learn about politics and history.

What the revolutionary leader hadn't counted on was that Saima had learned too well. Visits to the new library that King Khadduri had recently opened had convinced the revolutionary that the Polisario Front was worse than the problem it proposed to cure. Saima had contacted the secret police and had been asked to provide information directly to the king himself, a job he was glad to perform, especially since he was being paid for it.

Faluja *would* be stopped, Saima thought, watching the leader pace across the room, his words droning on monotonously. Now that Saima had the name of the general involved in the plot, he had the ammunition he needed to derail the whole movement.

His mind returned to Faluja for a moment since the tone of the leader's voice was changing.

"Therefore," the revolutionary leader was saying, "I am going to have all of you stay here tonight. We cannot risk your being questioned by the police. A traffic accident, a marital dispute, or anything else involving the police could ruin our plans. So we will stay here until tomorrow morning."

Saima sat miserably, trying to think of a way to get the name of the traitorous general to the king.

CHAPTER

25

The lone MH-60K hung above the churning dust clouds, floating serenely above the boiling sea of sand that scoured the desert below. The vehicle's shadow bobbed on the chaos that totally blotted out the surface of the desert.

"There they are," Death Song said, gazing at his multi-mode radar screen. "Only four. They're having to stay above the storm so they don't damage their engines. It's forced them to fly high enough that we're able to detect them on our radar."

In the distance, Oz could barely discern the images of the jets as they sparkled in the heat waves above the dust storm.

"Time to play decoy," Oz told his crew. He kicked the rudder pedal, inducing the chopper to twist in the sky. Then he pushed the control column forward to propel them away from the oncoming jets at the MH-60K's top speed.

"Arm our weapons," the pilot ordered Death Song. "The usual: give me the rockets and machine gun. Get the TOW up and be ready with the countermeasures pod." Oz triggered his radio. "Desert Six and Three, how're you doing down there?"

"One hell of a storm," the pilot of Desert Six replied. "Visibility is a big fat zero."

The two choppers rested on a rocky plateau, their engines turned off to prevent the sand from choking their filters.

"We're reading the jets on the backscatter from your radar," Desert Three radioed. "Looks like they're activating their radar as well. We won't have trouble telling when they've passed. Over."

"Come up as soon as they pass," Oz ordered. "They're gaining fast and will be playing for keeps."

"That's a roger, One."

Oz wiped the sweat from his forehead with his left hand, then grasped the collective pitch lever again, continuing south.

"The jets are gaining on us," Death Song warned.

"Desert One, this is Desert Three," the radio crackled. "They're passing us now. We're starting our engines. You'd better keep your head up because they've really got the afterburners going. We're—"

Static interrupted the transmission as the Mirage IIIs engaged their electronic jamming circuitry.

Oz pulled on the collective pitch lever, guiding his helicopter upward to take advantage of the MH-60K's ability to climb more swiftly than the jets. The maneuver shoved everyone in the chopper into their seats with the G-force.

"They're breaking formation," Death Song

warned, still watching the radar. "Trying to cut us off if we head at right angles in either direction."

"Desert One," the radio called. The rest of the message was drowned out by static.

"Say again," Oz called.

"Desert One," the voice on the radio repeated. "This is Three. I say again, our engines will not start!"

Oz swore under his breath. "Desert Six, how are you doing?"

There was a hiss, then Desert Six cut through the jamming. "We've got trouble. The damned sand. Hang on . . ." There was another wave of static.

"Looks like we're on our own," Oz announced over the intercom. "It's too late to outrun them. We'll take as many as we can."

The American pilot continued to lift his chopper, kicking his right pedal as he pulled on the control column to slow their speed. He faced the helicopter toward the four incoming jets.

"Fire as soon as they're in range," Oz directed Death Song. "I'll keep it steady." With only two TOWs and no backup from the other choppers, the pilot knew they'd be lucky to down even one of the jets. Oz silently cursed the events that had turned the American ambush into a trap.

"Launching the first TOW," Death Song said. "The other planes will be on top of us before I can launch the second."

"Just concentrate on your target," Oz ordered his co-pilot. "At least we'll get one of 'em."

The TOW blooped from its tube and its engine coughed to life.

As the missile shot toward the jets, Oz fired the last of his rockets from their pod. While the chance of hitting one of the jets with an unguided rocket was remote, he hoped the maneuver might force one or more of the oncoming Mirages off their course to give Death Song time to launch a second TOW.

The radio hissed and whistled with static. "We're in the air and have the two bandits on the east covered," Desert Six announced.

O.T. whooped with joy as Death Song's TOW reached its target. The missile ripped into the cockpit of the plane, instantly killing the Libyan pilot. The jet dropped out of control in a steep dive that hurtled it into the sandstorm below.

A fire-and-forget Hellfire missile on Desert Six blossomed to life as the AH-64 Apache poked through the dust clouds. The seven-inch diameter rocket quickly accelerated, chasing after one of the jets.

The gunner in the AH-64 didn't wait for the Hellfire to find its mark. He swiftly launched two more of the deadly weapons, targeting each with his nose laser.

The Hellfires locked onto the three remaining jets.

The planes banked, trying to lose the oncoming missiles, with two of the jets twisting and climbing; the electronic circuits in the Hellfire automatically compensated for their movements and continued to home toward the targets.

Within seconds, two Hellfires hit their marks.

One of the Mirages exploded in a spectacular blast that shattered it into metal confetti. The larger chunks of debris created by the explosion tumbled through the atmosphere, their flat surfaces reflecting the evening sunlight like polished glass.

The other Hellfire struck the triangular wing of its target. The plane wheeled in a tight circle, out of control, as the pilot bailed out. His parachute was instantly caught by the wind and he was dragged downward into the sandstorm.

The final Mirage tried a desperate maneuver as the Hellfire gained on it; the pilot dived into the dust storm, the missile streaking toward his tail.

"Smart," Oz remarked, watching the plane vanish.

"We've still got him on radar," Death Song said. "It looks like he lost the missile."

The pilot glanced toward the screen. "He's coming right at us!" He jerked the control column backward, throwing the helicopter's tail down and backing them up.

The Mirage thundered out of the sandstorm less than forty feet ahead. Oz hit the fire button on his control column, kicking his left rudder pedal simultaneously. The nose of the helicopter whipped around, keeping the Mirage in front of its guns for an extra moment as the jet hissed by ahead of them, rocking the helicopter with its wake.

As the Mirage escaped from Oz's sight picture faster than the helicopter could turn, O.T. lashed out with his Minigun. He, too, quit firing as the jet hurtled away.

"Think we did any damage?" Oz asked.

"There's your answer," Death Song replied.

The canopy of the jet ripped upward and the pilot ejected, riding the rocket under his seat upward to gain altitude before his parachute opened. Two seconds later, the pilotless Mirage exploded in midair.

The radio crackled as Oz rotated his helicopter around to see Desert Three rising out of the sandstorm.

"Desert Three, nice of you to join us," Oz razzed the other chopper crew.

"Sorry about that, chief," the Desert Three pilot answered in a perfect imitation of Maxwell Smart.

26

Bhaliq twinkled in the early evening darkness, its palace highlighted in a blaze of electric floodlights. Stacy Stallworth, standing before a panoramic view of the North African capital, watched her sound man signal five seconds, moistened her lips, and gazed directly into the TV camera's unblinking eye as the red light stared back at her.

"Good evening from Bhaliq, East Sahra," she began. "Rumors continue to spread in East Sahra tonight as stories about mutilated bodies in the desert and unarmed Bedouin villagers claiming to have been attacked by American personnel continue to surface.

"In the U.S.," Stallworth read, as technicians halfway around the world readied their tape, "Senator Francis Higgins has demanded that the U.S. leave East Sahra."

The tape showing the senator's diatribe replaced the reporter's live feed. In fifteen seconds, the director gave Stallworth a five second warning that the tape was coming to an end.

"One thing is certain," Stallworth resumed, ignoring the fly that buzzed around her notes. "A civil war is becoming more likely with each passing hour, as Prince Sulaiman remains in the hands of unknown kidnappers and King Khadduri's twenty-four hour deadline for the return of his son grows near.

"Sources inside the military fear open revolts by the minority tribes—the Qahidi, Sa'adi, and Banu Hilals," she said, checking her notes.

"In the meantime, King Abdul Karim Khadduri, himself a member of the majority Tuareg tribe, has scheduled a press conference for tomorrow morning. Sources close to the palace have admitted that this will be his declaration of war if his son has not been returned.

"Critics of the ruler caution that the monarch's impatience may actually hinder his son's return and play into the hands of the kidnappers. But the king appears to be determined to maintain his deadline.

"Only one thing is certain—tomorrow promises to be a day of reckoning for the little African kingdom of East Sahra."

The reporter smiled at the camera as the segment came to an end. "For CCN, this is Stacy Stallworth in Bhaliq, East Sahra."

The sunset evolved into darkness as the three Night Stalkers helicopters passed above the desert storm.

"We're exhausting our fuel," Oz told Warner over the COMSAT link. "And it's a sure bet the storm has obliterated the camel tracks we were following. Any suggestions? Over."

Warner hesitated, "That's a good question. Do you have enough fuel to get into Morocco?"

"Negative on that," Oz replied. "We could just make Bhaliq if we started right now."

"I suppose that's what should be done," the commander said, "but given the leaks and the two jet attacks that resulted, I'm not too crazy about directing you into the capital. What would you think of hunkering down and waiting for something to break?"

"When in doubt, wait it out?" Oz asked.

"Something like that," Warner answered. "It's possible that whoever has the prince may be trying to send a message after they've reached their destination. If the NSA intercepted it, it could be the break we need. If nothing comes of that, we can always airlift fuel to you and get you out before a civil war erupts. Over."

"How about if we set down in the storm, button up, and stay hidden for a while?" Oz said. "We'd conserve on fuel and be in the neighborhood if anything turns up. I hate sitting around with the clock running out, but I guess there's not much else we can do right now. Over."

"That sounds reasonable," Warner agreed.

"Is there any word on Luger? Over."

Warner was silent a moment. "Luger's in real bad shape," he finally said. "I'll let you know if his condition changes."

"He's not dead, is he? You'd level with me if he were."

"Of course I would," Warner growled. "What do you think I am? He's in bad shape—we've transferred him to West Germany. So he's got the best medical care available.

"Now get some rest," Warner ordered the pilot. "I'll contact you if we get anything on the prince. If the NSA doesn't deliver, then I'll call in four hours. Over and out."

Oz switched his radio to the ABN ultra-high frequency and spoke to the other two choppers flying beside him. "Looks like the sandstorm's nearly expended itself," he said. "We're going to land on the plateau. We'll sit tight for a while and hope intelligence can give us a lead. In the meantime, let's get as much rest as we can."

The choppers slowly descended into the desert storm, the pilots using their radar to locate good landing positions and to avoid crashing into each other.

"Shut her off," Oz directed Death Song after landing on the rocky surface of the plateau. The pilot stared through the Plexiglass windscreen; the landing lights, reflecting off the swirling dirt, gave the pilot the claustrophobic feeling of being underwater rather than in an aircraft. He promptly switched them off.

The engines wound down and abruptly there was stillness broken only by the whistling of the wind and the patter of the sand on the surface of the aircraft.

"I'll take the first watch," Oz told Death Song.

"Thanks," the co-pilot yawned. He removed his helmet and settled into the bucket seat, propping his booted feet on top of the control pedals.

"O.T.," Oz called on the intercom.

"Yes, sir," a tired voice answered.

"Have Jaber tell the Bedouins we're probably going to be here for a few hours and to get as comfortable as they can. If anyone needs to leave the chopper and answer nature's call, they shouldn't wander more than a few yards in case we need to leave in a hurry."

"That's a roger."

Qaim watched as the Bedouin chief cut the ropes binding Prince Sulaiman. When he had finished, the prince smiled as the chief bowed. "If you'll excuse me, I have a radio call I need to make," the prince explained, rubbing his wrists.

"But—" Qaim sputtered, finding himself at a loss for words.

The prince grinned and stopped to explain. "It was all a sham, my friend. We didn't want the peace conference to succeed. Even the West understands the need for vengeance and justice. When my father announces to the press that I have been slain, the world may not cheer him on as he slaughters his opposition, but it will understand. Don't worry," he assured Qaim with a smile, "You will be paid for your work."

King Khadduri activated the radio, pushing his mistress away. "Get dressed!" he ordered. She pouted pertly and slunk away with an exaggerated sway of her hips.

"Yes," he spoke into the mouthpiece.

"We reached our hideout just before the sandstorm hit," Prince Sulaiman's voice came over the speaker. "I hope you're going to get the troops to us soon," he said. "I hate sitting here with just a pack of Bedouin horsemen and a handful of assassins guarding me."

"The troops will be there after the storm passes," the king reassured him. "I handpicked them myself. The trick was getting the planes out from under General Mahala's nose."

"How is our national hero?"

"You would have been very moved at how he carried on when he thought he'd found your body," the monarch snorted. "That gave me a start as well, however."

"You can't get rid of me that easily. Do you think the general suspects anything?"

"No. He's been working night and day trying to find you. I'm going to have trouble getting him to do the job at hand. By the way, I discovered who tried to blow us up."

"Who?"

"The Polisario Front. We've captured the man that carried out the bombing—our informant fingered him. I'll arrest the rest of them tomorrow before they can do any more damage."

"It's hard to believe they have enough power to pose a danger."

"Never underestimate a political entity that has the good of the people as its goal," the king cautioned. "Our informant says Faluja—their leader—is working for one of our generals who is ready to usurp control after we've been assassinated."

"We need to take care of the general before the war of retribution," the prince suggested.

"I hope to have General Mahala arrest the wayward officer shortly," the king answered. "My informant is trying to uncover his identity now. Then, after Mahala has destroyed the minority tribes, we will get rid of him, too. He could be the last victim of the Polisario Front, perhaps."

Sulaiman nodded. "That's a good idea. Listen, father, I better go now. My babysitters are beginning to look bored."

"Enjoy your rest, Sulaiman. There will be plenty to do after the civil war has begun to avenge your kidnapping."

"Good night."

The sovereign turned off the radio.

High above him, the SIGINT satellite silently mulled over the signal, processed it, and relayed the data on the long trip toward the NSA computers.

Saima shivered in the night air seeping through the cracks and open windows of the mud hut. He carefully rose from his hard cot, eyeing the dark forms around him, and wondered if they were really asleep.

He waited a full minute, listening to the heavy snoring and deep breathing of the sleeping men. Should anyone wake and challenge him, Saima had prepared an excuse about needing to relieve himself.

The informant carefully stepped over Gamal Faluja, briefly speculating to himself about what type of mad dreams the revolutionary must have.

The Arab paused at the front door and removed

the heavy crossbar that served as its lock. The splintery wood scraped along the iron hooks holding the shaft in place. Saima heard his heart thumping as he finally set the bar on the dirt floor.

The Bedouin stared into the darkness, trying to discern any movement among the prone figures in the room, when suddenly Faluja restlessly rolled over onto his back.

A ripple coursed along Saima's spine while his hand snaked toward his dagger.

Oh, Allah, help your stupid, ignorant child who is about to be slaughtered, he prayed silently.

But Faluja didn't rise, shout, or do anything other than resume snoring.

The informant released his breath and slowly opened the door, thankful it didn't turn on squeaking hinges. He stepped outside and quietly shut the door behind himself, glancing up and down the narrow street.

Saima grasped the dagger with his right hand while his left checked the folds in his clothing. He located the one-dirham coins in the leather purse concealed in the sash of his *kumsan.*

Observing no one on the street, he hurried through the shadows, glancing over his shoulder periodically to be sure he wasn't being followed. Suddenly, he spied a stopped old man rounding the corner ahead, limping toward him.

The informer tensed; the pedestrian appeared harmless enough, but Saima couldn't afford trouble. He crossed to the other side of the street, and sighed with relief as the two passed without incident.

As he hastened toward his destination, the dark

street seemed ominously quiet; not one but thieves and cutthroats are out-of-doors at this hour, Saima thought.

After what seemed an eternity, the informant finally rounded a mud hut and saw what he was searching for. Ahead, bathed in its own pool of light, was the metal box encasing the one pay-phone for miles around.

Saima paused, studying the street.

He hated going to the phone booth—it was so exposed. Finally, he wiped the sweat from palms and tightly grasped the dagger.

He crossed the narrow street and stood under the light shining on the booth, aware that if Faluja had followed, he'd have no trouble identifying the caller.

As his shaky fingers extracted the purse from his sash, he fumbled with the cords and finally retrieved a coin. He paused thinking he heard a sandled foot scrape the dry earth.

He turned to stare up and down the street. No one.

Grabbing the phone from its cradle and holding it between his shoulder and cheek, he heard the dial tone and shoved the coin into the slot. He dialed the king's private number.

The phone rang once.

Twice.

"Hello," the voice of the potentate's aide, el-Kaukji, answered.

"I must talk to the king," Saima whispered.

"Who is this?"

"Saima. I must talk to—"

"One moment. I'm not sure where he is, but I will get him."

Saima waited impatiently. Thinking he heard footsteps, he turned hastily and scanned down the street.

There is no one, he chided himself. Your nerves will get the best of you yet, you fool.

"He'll be here in a minute," el-Kaukji said over the phone. "Tell me the message."

"General Saad el-Sid is the one working for the Polisario Front," Saima whispered urgently. "The king must—"

"General el-Sid?"

"Yes!" Hearing footsteps again, Saima turned but saw no one in the thick shadows.

"He's working for the Polisario Front?" el-Kaukji asked.

There was no answer.

After trying repeatedly to get a response, el-Kaukji finally hung up. Standing in the king's office, the aide hesitated a moment, then decided to take the short message to King Khadduri at once.

In the dark street at the edge of town, Faluja replaced the pay-phone on its cradle, wondering how much Saima had revealed of the Polisario Front's plans and to whom he had divulged them.

He wiped the blade of his knife on the traitor's robe, earnestly hoping that the revolution was still on schedule.

The wind shook the MH-60K, showering it with dirt. Oz turned around in his seat and looked into the gunners compartment.

O.T. was quietly playing a game of chess with one of the Qahidi, using a tiny ivory and wood set the Bedouin had produced from his pack. The pilot was surprised at first to see the chess set, then remembered having heard somewhere that the Arabs had actually invented the game, bringing it into Europe during the moorish skirmishes of the Middle Ages.

The American momentarily eyed the Bedouin sitting in Luger's chair and was reminded of the young gunner who would normally have been seated there. Oz thought back to that week long ago when he, O.T., Death Song, and Luger had first worked together.

It had been a bad scene, he remembered.

The helicopter team had been thrown together, none of them knowing each other and none of them getting along. Death Song was slow to produce data for Oz on the HSD; Luger and O.T. were always talking on the intercom at the same time, making it impossible for anyone to communicate. What should have been a crack helicopter team was instead coming in last during field exercises.

To be fair, Oz admitted to himself, much of the problem had been him. He wasn't accustomed to the new controls. He was more familiar with the Huey, and the new "hi-tech" system the MH-60K utilized just wasn't like the "six-pack" dials and gauges of the older machine, even if the modern ones were supposed to be easier to master.

So, by the third day of the exercise, everyone was depressed.

"How 'bout gettin' together at Bill's Ranch

House Saloon?" O.T. suggested as the four crew-men climbed out of the MH-60K.

"I don't know," Luger said.

"They've got a good band and the food's great," O.T. said. "I'll spring for the first round of drinks. It's out on Pine Haven Road by the munici-pal airport."

Death Song raised an eyebrow and said noth-ing.

"Oh, come on, you guys," O.T. chided. "Don't be a bunch of stick-in-the-muds."

"Okay, I'm game," Luger yielded, looking more than ever like a high-school kid instead of a soldier.

As it turned out, O.T.'d never been to the dive before, and the band had played the raunchiest country-western music Oz had ever heard. But O.T. regaled everybody with a bunch of old army stories and, after a few beers, the four airmen were having a pretty good time.

They were getting ready to leave at about eleven, when five rednecks carrying pool cues ap-proached the table.

"Howdy," O.T. said amiably, placing a healthy tip on the table for the flirtatious waitress. "How's it going?"

The muscular fellow in the lead ignored O.T.'s pleasantry, speaking instead to Death Song, "Me and my friends here was wondering if you was a wetback or a stinking Indian?" he demanded.

"Look," Oz said, rising to his feet, "we're leav-ing. We don't want any trouble."

The leader turned to Oz. "We want to know if

your colored friend here is a red face or a wetback," the bully persisted, his buddies bunching up around him, holding their pool cues like ball bats.

Death Song smiled and said evenly, "I'm an American just like you. Maybe more so since my people have been here longer."

"No you ain't," the rowdy declared, brandishing his pool cue. "And we don't like your kind in our bar."

"Hey, are you the owner of this establishment?" Luger asked innocently, turning in his chair to look up at the ruffian. "I've got something you're supposed to have. Glad you reminded me."

The rowdy was taken off balance by the question. Before he could think of an answer, Luger grabbed his shirt collar and jerked downward with all his might, smashing the man's face into the table top.

Oz punched the nearest troublemaker, at the same time grabbing the rowdy's pool cue with his free hand to use it as a weapon. Simultaneously, O.T. hit one of the other five in the nose with the heavy beer mug he'd grabbed off the table.

The skirmish lasted less than thirty seconds. The five thugs were left lying on the floor unconscious or wishing they were; the four airmen exited before anyone could initiate another attack or call the police.

O.T. drove them to the emergency room of the HSA Cumberland Hospital. "We don't want to use the base medics," the warrant officer explained, slowing the car in front of the four-story building.

"Yeah," Luger laughed, "they might think we'd been in a fight."

"It was more like an ambush than a fight," Death Song grinned. "That was some move, Luger. You guys saved my hide."

"One for all and all for one," the youthful Luger declared.

"Not too original," O.T. chuckled, "but it'll do. Maybe we could have it translated into Latin."

Seventeen stitches later, the four airmen returned to Fort Bragg on the north side of Fayetteville. Although physically worse off for their outing, they were a team thereafter, both on the ground and in the air.

Oz's attention was drawn to the on-board computer as it locked onto the download sign from the COMSAT circling the earth high above the desert.

I hope Warner's got some leads, the pilot thought to himself, switching on the radio.

CHAPTER

27

"So I think we have the lead we were looking for," Warner reported to Oz over the COMSAT. "The NSA intercepted a broadcast coming from forty kilometers southeast of you at the coordinates I gave you."

Oz studied the CRT display. "About the only thing of interest in that area is an old mine."

"An abandoned salt mine," Warner said. "Probably a good place to start your search."

"That's a pretty big area, considering we don't have much time." He checked his watch. "Just three hours till the king's deadline for the return of his son."

"The conversation intercepted by the NSA is somewhat garbled," Warner told Oz. "But the gist is that the prince is responsible for his own disappearance."

"That's going to make it real hard to get him out of there," Oz thought aloud.

"And according to the intercept, the king seems to be planning an all-out attack on the other three tribes."

"I guess first we'd better find the prince and then we'll worry about how to return him to Bhaliq," Oz decided. "The storm's clearing here and is headed toward the hideout. If we follow it in, that might give us some cover."

"That would probably be best," Warner agreed.

"Couldn't the information about the royal family's treachery be leaked to the press?" Oz queried.

"We considered that," Warner admitted. "But the State Department won't buy it. We're already at the edge trying to convince Congress and the press we're not getting into another Vietnam."

"How do they figure that?"

"You wouldn't believe the press stories. Your battle at Fort Danjou and the dispute with the Qahidi have taken on epic proportions. It would be funny if it weren't so pathetic."

"Then we'll have to produce the prince," Oz concluded. "That would scuttle the king's excuse for attacking the other tribes, even if both royals deny faking the kidnapping."

"I'm afraid that's the only way."

"We'd better get a move on," Oz said. "Fuel's going to be our big problem since we'll be headed away from Bhaliq."

"We have a KC-135R Stratotanker en route to you now," Warner advised. ETA for your area is two hours. With any luck, you can refuel and make it to the capital before the press conference."

"Anything else?"

"That's it. I'll keep this channel open. Let me know when you're in the air. Over and out."

Oz switched his radio to the ABN frequency and contacted the other chopper crews. "We need to get going," he urged after apprising them of the situation and giving them their new coordinates. "I'm hoping we can follow the tail end of the storm all the way to the mines. We'll travel in standard trail formation. Six, you'll take the lead with Three behind you. I'll bring up the rear. Any questions?"

"This is Lieutenant Victor," the Delta Force leader called from Desert Three. "Do you have any idea exactly where the prince is hidden? Our maps show that as being a pretty good-sized place."

"That's a negative on the location, lieutenant. The NSA couldn't narrow it by more than a few miles. Your guys will have to search on the ground while we cover the air. If we get in undetected, we'll probably drop you off and let you hoof it in on foot so our engine noise doesn't alert them. I'm hoping we'll get lucky with our NVGs and FLIRs, but we'll have to wing it for the most part."

"What type of resistance can we expect?" asked the pilot of Desert Six.

"That's another unknown," Oz replied. "Commander Warner said the communique indicated the East Sahran planes coming in after the storm. So there may be aircraft to contend with if we don't get in ahead of them."

There was silence over the radio.

"Gentlemen," Oz said. "Time is of the essence; let's get a move on."

Shortly, the Delta Force troops, Bedouin tribesmen, and air crews were ready for take off. The engines of the helicopters started with low roars that increased in volume, rocking the plateau. Miniature tornadoes of sand engulfed the three machines as they rose, strobe lights flashing to help the pilots avoid hitting each other.

Oz raised his helicopter and gracefully fell in behind the AH-64 and the other MH-60K. The helicopters flew low in the starry night, using their TF/TA radar to avoid detection by the East Sahran military. They traveled at their maximum air speed of 290 kilometers per hour, which would deliver them to the salt mine in a few minutes.

Oz switched his radio to Warner's COMSAT frequency. "Desert Hen, your chicks are away," he reported.

"Desert Hen reads you loud and clear," Warner said from his command post halfway around the world. "Good luck. Over and out."

The Boeing KC-135R Stratotanker cruised at 30,000 feet, its four F10-8-CF-100 turbofan engines creating a dull roar that the pilot, Major James Dugan, found comforting.

Lieutenant John Mowinski, his co-pilot, handed Dugan a steaming cup of coffee.

"Thanks," Dugan deadpanned. "Maybe this will help keep me awake while I stare at the autopilot." He glanced at the electronic cruise control located below the throttles on the console between him and the co-pilot.

"You still awake Morgan?" the pilot asked his flight engineer.

"Awake," Lieutenant Morgan, announced from his chair aft of the co-pilot. His job was to monitor the various systems on the plane, including the electronic, hydraulic, and fuel management operations of the aircraft. "Everything is operating in the green."

"You've got to get more sleep while we're on the ground," Dugan chided the flight engineer. "You've got dark circles under your eyes you could trip over."

"And she was worth every minute of it," the lieutenant chuckled.

"How's the radar look?" Dugan inquired of his co-pilot as Mowinski settled into his chair to the right of the pilot.

Lieutenant Mowinski studied the scope. "We still have the two commercials over the Mediterranean."

Dugan studied the inertial navigation system display. "Looks like we're about fifteen minutes away from Algerian airspace," he said. "I'd better double check with them to be sure they know we're heading in."

"Hang on," Mowinski said, staring at the radar scope to the lower left of his control panel.

"What've you got?" Dugan asked.

"Something's coming up real fast from the east."

"Coming in our direction?"

"Yeah. It's rising to our altitude, too. Three jets. They've got to be fighters, as fast as they're traveling."

Dugan swore under his breath and quickly downed the coffee. "I'm taking us off auto," he announced. The pilot pulled the wheel toward him, inducing the plane to climb higher. "Max altitude and max speed, too. Let's see if these guys are really serious or just jocking around."

The engines thundered to a higher pitch that carried through the steel airframe of the KC-135R.

"They're still gaining on us and climbing," Lieutenant Mowinski warned.

The crew was quiet.

Mowinski yelled, "They're locking onto us with targeting radar!"

Major Dugan cursed and jerked the mask on his helmet around to cover his face. He spoke into the radio mike in the mask. "This is KC-54 calling unidentified aircraft on course heading—"

"They're firing missiles!" the co-pilot cried.

Major Dugan forced the plane into a steep dive, banking to the west. Several long seconds passed as the pilot's maneuver seemed to gain enough speed for the KC-135R to out-distance one of the missiles.

"Major, they're launching another salvo!" Mowinski alerted the pilot.

"We've got to get the COMSAT and let our people know what's happening," Dugan muttered, flipping the switch on the computerized radio.

"They're coming in fast," Mowinski warned. "They're right on us!"

The pilot guided the wheel to the left, attempting to alter their course fast enough to elude the missiles. He prepared to speak over the radio, but before he could make the call, one of the missiles connected.

The fuel in the tanker ignited, lighting up the sky with its brilliant yellow fireball.

The wreckage of the American tanker rained onto the northern coast of Algeria. As it fell, the three fighter jets wheeled around and returned to Libya.

CHAPTER

28

King Khadduri glanced at his alarm clock. It was still two-and-a-half hours before his scheduled press conference. Who was beating on his door?

He kicked one leg from under the silk sheets, and sat listening to the soft rap on the door. His mistress stirred and rolled over in the bed. The monarch noted she was gaining a little weight and momentarily wondered if it was time to get a new playmate. He scratched his hairy chest and plodded through the large dressing room adjoining the bedroom and pulled the door open.

"I'm sorry to bother you, your Excellency," el-Kaukji said. "But Saima called."

The three American choppers traveled through the murky desert night, following the tail of the sandstorm rolling to the south. In the passenger compartment of Oz's MH-60K, Sergeant Young showed the Bedouin warriors how to use the spare NVG the chopper carried.

"Like this," he shouted, helping Izaak adjust the device. "This turns it on."

Jaber translated what the American had said and the Qahidi chief smiled and nodded.

Sergeant Young was surprised at how quickly the Bedouins learned to operate the equipment. "If all the newbies in the Army did this well, they wouldn't need sergeants," he cracked to Zeller. The sergeant paused to spit tobacco into the tin can he was holding, then continued his instructions to the Bedouins. "Now be sure to switch them off until we get there. Like this. Otherwise the batteries run down and they're a bitch to change."

The Bedouins watched intently in the dimly-lit interior of the chopper. Then each expertly switched off his NVG.

"If these guys fight half as well as they learn," the Sergeant muttered to Jaber, "then they're going to kick some ass when we get to the salt mines."

"They are very good fighters," Jaber answered. "Though I'm not sure about kicking donkeys."

Young grinned. "I'm sure they'll do just fine."

In the cabin of the chopper, sand rattled against the windscreen of the MH-60K.

"Better slow down, Desert Six and Three," Oz radioed. "We seem to have caught up with the storm."

"We're getting close to the SP," Death Song cautioned.

Oz checked the horizontal situation display that showed the map projection and navigation reference points updated by the 1750A/J73 dual mission computers. Then he glanced at the fuel and power management format. "We won't have much fuel to

maneuver with once we get there," he told Death
Song.

The TF/TA automatically took them upward
over the cliffs ahead. Once they had cleared the hills,
they followed the alluvial fans that grew into huge
deposits of rock, sand, and gravel at the base of the
mountain arroyo that led to the playa where the salt
mine sat.

Oz glanced at the map, switched to his ABN
UHF channel, and spoke to the other aircraft ahead
of him in the trail formation. "Here's our SP," he
announced. "Let's keep our pattern low and tight.
Arm your weapons."

The helicopters followed the twisting route of
a second arroyo snaking below them.

Death Song finished throwing the switches that
armed the MH-60K's weapons pods. "Weapons are
armed," he announced. "Usual configuration, but
only one TOW and no seven-and-a-halfs."

"O.T.," Oz called. "Arm your Minigun."

"Mini armed," O.T. answered.

"Sergeant Young, better get your men ready
and tell the Bedouins we're about there."

"That's a roger," Young's voice answered
around a wad of tobacco.

"That our ACP?" queried the pilot of the AH-
64.

"That's it," Death Song informed Oz, eyeing
the dry stream bed that twisted into a near circle,
forming a readily recognized landmark for the fliers.

Oz toggled the radio. "That's affirmative," he
replied, following the two shadowy shapes of the
helicopters ahead of him. The three aircraft vectored

eastward, hugging the dry stream bed that fed into the alkaline crater of the salt mine.

"Radar is clear and there're no radio transmissions other than our own," Death Song reported to Oz. "RP coming up."

"Sergeant Young," Oz said over the intercom. "We're at the release point and heading in."

"We're ready," Young said glancing at the Bedouins. The fighters were an odd contrast of new and old, with bandoliers of 7.62mm cartridges for their modern Heckler & Koch G3 rifles, NVGs over their turbans, and short swords and daggers in their belts.

The sergeant removed his intercom headset and yelled above the engine noise to Jaber, "We're headed in."

"Headed in?" the translator asked.

"Landing!" Young hollered, spitting the last of his tobacco into the can and raising his night vision goggles to his face. "Ready?" he shouted to his three Delta Force Troops.

Zeller signaled a thumbs up, then cycled a cartridge into the sniper rifle that again sported a night vision scope.

Young double-checked the safety on his Colt Model 610 carbine and twisted the knob on the electronic Aimpoint scope in its carrying handle; he lifted it up to inspect the glowing dot reticle, then tested the fastener on the Bowie knife strapped to his combat vest.

"Desert Six," Oz called over the radio from the cockpit of the MH-60K, "we're landing. Take your satellite position."

"Will do, One," the pilot of the AH-64 radioed. The gunship started the wide circle that would allow it to search for hazards in the area surrounding the landing site for the two MH-60Ks.

Desert Three flew ahead of Oz, dropping to the gravelly floor of the dry creek bed and blowing up a storm of dust as it neared the ground. Oz dropped his chopper behind the landing MH-60K as the squad inside Desert Three leaped from its side doors.

He landed in a white-out, bobbing on the hydraulic landing gear; within seconds, O.T. called out, "They're all off."

The Bedouins and Delta Force troops ran clear of the second MH-60K as Oz lifted it into the air. The men joined the other Delta Force troopers running toward the salt mine.

"Looks like we have company," Death Song warned the pilot as they climbed into the air. "Six bandits coming fast out of the north."

Gamal Faluja awoke an hour-and-a-half before the scheduled press conference, a battered mechanical alarm clock jangling him out of his restless sleep.

He exchanged his stained *kumsan* for the brown jumpsuit that had provided him safe passage into the hotel before. There was no reason to think it wouldn't work again.

This time, Faluja promised himself, I'll kill the tyrant.

"Wait for my return," he instructed the three revolutionaries, deciding to leave them behind lest others in the group prove to be traitors.

He exited the hut with the long box containing his rifle and trekked on foot for nearly a mile to an empty mud shack. After studying the area briefly, he crossed the street, unlocked the huge gate on the building, and pulled it open. The he walked in and climbed into the stolen delivery truck parked inside.

Within minutes Faluja was parking the vehicle in a loading zone in front of the hotel. "There is a problem with your phones," he explained to the aged doorman who admitted the revolutionary with a cursory inspection of his stolen ID cards.

Faluja rode the delivery elevator to the fifth floor, got off, and when he was sure no one was watching, pushed his way through the wooden doors leading to the stairwell. He quietly and cautiously climbed the five flights to the top of the building.

The revolutionary stepped onto the roof, and slowly pivoting, took in a panoramic view of the sleeping city. Then he spied the palace in the distance and Faluja's mood soured perceptibly. He decided to get to the task at hand.

After setting the box down on the tar roof, he unfastened the string holding it together and opened the flaps. The cloth-wrapped rifle slid out of its container.

Faluja removed the cloth and stroked the oiled wooden stock of the scoped rifle. Then he pulled the bolt open and retrieved the brass cartridges from the box. He carefully inserted the cartridges, one at a time, into the firearm's magazine. The bolt slammed closed as he pushed forward on its lever, chambering a round.

The revolutionary crossed to the edge of the flat

roof, taking care to stay in the shadows and keeping low to avoid being silhouetted against the sky. He stopped at the edge and studied the dimly-lit platform where the king would speak an hour after the sun rose. Smiling to himself, Faluja shouldered the gun and sighted on the wooden podium.

As he lowered the rifle, his neck and skull exploded.

The counter sniper atop the building across the road lowered his bullpup rifle, a sick feeling in the pit of his stomach. Seeing the three heavy, subsonic slugs reach the target was the worst part of his assignment.

"You got him," the sniper's observer said in Arabic, studying the nearly headless corpse lying on the rooftop across the street. "Let me inspect the other buildings, then I'll call to have the body bagged."

The Bedouin sniper closed his eyes a moment. Then he checked the heavy silencer that had lowered the muzzle blast from his AUG HBAR-T rifle to a popping sound that hadn't even disturbed any of the press corps sleeping in the hotel.

The sniper snapped the cross-bolt safety on the left of the rifle's handguard to the right and glanced at his observer, who swept the buildings encircling them with binoculars. "See anyone else?" the sniper asked.

"No, it looks clear. That must've been the only one."

The sniper hoped there were no more. He didn't enjoy his job, even though he tried to reassure

himself that it was necessary—after all there was no
doubt the gunman was planning to shoot the king.
Despite the justification, the Bedouin soldier still felt
sick about what he'd done.

29

"Have they detected us?" Oz asked.

"I don't think so," Death Song answered. "They just appeared over the ridge. I don't think they could pick us out of the clutter of these rock formations."

"Desert One, this is Six. We've got some blips."

"Roger, we got 'em too," Oz radioed. "They must be the aircraft the king was sending to guard the prince. Let's see if we can take them before they reach the salt mines. Six, we'll have a tailless diamond formation with you at the point. Three, you take the port side and we'll hang on starboard. Go in low so they can't detect us."

The three American choppers hugged the earth as they raced toward the oncoming planes.

"Slow to a stop," Oz ordered the choppers as the enemy aircraft approached. "We'll let them pass and then pop up and hit them. If these are V-22s, remember they can hover just like choppers. Don't let 'em fake you out. Over."

Oz and the other pilots held their choppers steady as the six airplanes drew near.

Suddenly the formation slowed.

"Have they spotted us?" Six called.

"Everyone sit tight," Oz ordered over the radio.

The formation of planes had come to a near standstill and, for a terrible moment, the Americans thought they'd been detected.

Then, just as suddenly, the six V-22s passed on by.

"Let's swing around into reverse formation," Oz radioed the two choppers. Three, you'll be on starboard. Six, move up after we're facing south. Then we'll attack. We have only one TOW left on this 'copter, so you guys will have to take up the slack for us. Six, gun for the center. Three, take the right."

"That's a roger, One," Six said.

"We read you," Three affirmed.

The three American helicopters rotated to follow the V-22s, rising as they turned.

"They're radioing each other," Death Song informed Oz. "I can't make out what they're saying—they're speaking Arabic. I'm ready on the TOW."

"Can you jam their radios with the countermeasure pod?"

"I'll give it a try."

As the co-pilot worked with his controls, the V-22s abruptly broke formation.

"They've seen us," Oz radioed to the other two choppers. "Fire at will."

Instantly a Hellfire missile raced away from the AH-64. The rocket's tail lit the desert night. The missile quickly accelerated toward its target as the gunner in the front of the Apache targeted a second V-22 with his laser designator.

"I'm launching," Death Song warned Oz as the chopper's last rocket tore out of its pod. In a blur of motion, its fins unfolded and its rocket kicked in.

As the Apache's Hellfire sought its target and connected, one of the V-22s exploded. A moment later, a second V-22's tail ripped apart as Desert Three's TOW found its target.

Death Song guided his missile in as two more Hellfires lit the sky with their exhaust. The V-22 Death Song stalked made a sharp bank, taking advantage of its ability to drop its air speed by rotating its twin blades upward.

But it didn't succeed in losing the TOW.

The missile hit the V-22's left engine, sending metal fragments into the hull next to the cockpit and instantly killing the pilot. The machine plunged to the earth, no longer aerodynamically stable. The impact hurled fragments far across the rocky plain. A fourth V-22 detonated as a Hellfire chased it down.

One of the two remaining Ospreys managed to elude an oncoming missile by diving toward the earth and then coming to a complete stop a few feet above the ground. As the Hellfire exploded in the rocks beyond the skillful pilot, the aircraft swung around and fired a salvo of unguided rockets at Desert Three.

The pilot of the MH-60K banked hard to the right to avoid the missiles, but one of the rockets entered the intake scoop of the chopper's left engine. The machine shuddered in the air, shrapnel from the explosion penetrating the gunners compartment and cockpit, instantly wounding the four crewmen.

The MH-60K whirled earthward, the pilot fighting to minimize the crash. His radio failed to respond as he tried to send a Mayday to his fellow pilots.

Oz watched the falling helicopter and swore, firing his guns at the other V-22, which was now turning toward him.

"They're locking onto us with targeting radar," Death Song warned. He hit several buttons on the countermeasure controls, attempting to send a false set of signals to the enemy missile's sensors.

The American pilot fired his dual machine guns and prepared to take evasive action. The first missile departed the V-22, and the bullets from the chopper's guns hit its warhead, detonating the rocket forty yards ahead of the MH-60K.

"Lucky shot," Oz muttered.

"They're locking onto us again," Death Song cautioned.

Before the V-22 could launch its missile, a Hellfire from Desert Six reached it, the rocket smashing into the tail of the aircraft and sending a fiery blast through the interior of its cabin. The Osprey shook as its rotors pulled against the weakened airframe. The damaged machine dropped to the earth while the wounded pilot tore at the stick, trying to regain control of his unresponsive airplane. The final V-22 skidded across the ground and broke apart.

Oz tried to reach Desert Three on his radio.

There was no reply.

"We're checking on Desert Three," Oz radioed the AH-64. "Satellite for us."

"That's a roger," the pilot of the AH-64 replied. "We'll ride shotgun."

"Keep it quiet," Lieutenant Victor ordered a trooper who had stumbled and cracked his knee against a rock, swearing loudly as he fell.

The private nodded sheepishly, biting his lip as he rose on the bruised leg.

The Americans and Bedouins had circled the perimeter of the dry lakebed with little problem, their NVGs enabling them to see in the darkness as they carefully picked their way through the rocks and deeply eroded earth. Nearing the salt mine's crater, Lieutenant Victor signaled a halt. Almost despairing at the immensity of the search area, he finally ordered his team down the well-traveled path leading into the crater. "Watch for booby traps," he warned.

As they were preparing to enter the ancient complex, Sergeant Young came jogging forward out of the shadows.

"Sir," Young said, "Look toward the east end of the valley. To the far left."

Victor looked where he'd been directed. There, its light magnified by the NVG, was the barely discernable glow of a cigarette.

"Good work," the lieutenant rejoiced, raising his hand to order another halt. Then Lieutenant Victor hastily devised a new plan to deploy his men as close to the cave entrance as possible without being detected.

30

General Saad el-Sid lay asleep in his bed when the noise of breaking glass awakened him. At first he thought he'd dreamed it; then he heard the footsteps in the hallway.

He reached for the Beretta Model 951 lying on the carved night table, turning his head from side to side to discern whether the shadow that didn't seem to belong in the room was an intruder. His fingers touched the 9mm pistol.

The shadowy figure lifted a Soviet-made Tokarev R-4 pistol, the weapon's discharge lighting the darkness as the .22 bullets left its muzzle. Three of the lead projectiles struck Saad el-Sid in the chest and neck.

The general's wife screamed as the gunman advanced toward the bed.

"I won't hurt you," he promised in Arabic. He placed the muzzle of the pistol he carried against the temple of the general, who lay struggling for breath and pulled the trigger.

The gunman reached across the body for the chain around the general's neck. He found the dog tags and yanked them off, breaking the silver chain that had been holding them in place.

With the general's ID tags in his possession, the gunman knew he would be able to collect the healthy reward the king had offered. The assassin replaced his weapon in its shoulder rig and quietly left the room, ignoring the weeping woman in the bed.

Oz landed his chopper while the AH-64 circled above, protecting them from a surprise attack. The flames from three of the wrecked V-22s flickered in the darkness, casting long shadows that appeared green in the pilot's NVG.

"I can check the chopper for survivors," O.T. volunteered over the intercom.

"Okay," Oz agreed. "We'll keep the engines running. Get the survivors on our 'copter if they can be moved. Be sure the chopper is destroyed if we can transfer the crew."

O.T. opened the side door and leaped out into the sand. He jogged over to the wrecked MH-60K, approaching it gingerly until he was certain its fuel tanks weren't ruptured. He yanked the pilot's door open.

"Didn't anyone ever tell you to knock?" the pilot inside wisecracked, dabbing at a cut on his forehead with a bandage from his combat vest.

"How are you guys?" O.T. asked, looking around the cockpit.

"Beat up but able to take care of ourselves," the pilot answered. "Our radio's shot and the chopper's totaled. Go ahead and take care of the Delta squad."

"Captain Carson would like to get you guys out of here. Can all of you walk to our chopper?"

The pilot spoke to his crew over the intercom. "Yeah, we can," he said,

While the four-man crew limped from Desert Three to Desert One, O.T. boarded the damaged helicopter. He jerked open the panel at the rear of the crew compartment and placed a white phosphorous grenade with a special timer on its top above the vehicle's self-sealing fuel cells.

He carefully set the timer for five minutes, then checked to be sure he could exit the crippled MH-60K quickly. He paused a second to take a deep breath and then pulled up the cover on the red arming button and pressed it, activating the timer.

The warrant officer vaulted out of the damaged aircraft and jogged to his own helicopter. Seconds later, he checked that the injured crew from the other chopper were fastened into their seats; then he plugged his helmet mike into the intercom. "She's set to blow and her crew is aboard our chopper," he reported.

Oz lifted the helicopter into the air. "Good job," he told his gunner.

Three minutes later the white phosphorous grenade ignited and the desert blazed with the explosion from the fuel tanks of the damaged MH-60K.

Lieutenant Victor had divided his men into two squads. The squad that consisted of the Sergeant Young's men and the eight Qahidi warriors headed around the rim of the salt mine's crater; the western cave near where the light had been spotted was their objective.

The second squad of Delta Force troops circled the crater from the east to cover the other twin cave.

Within fifteen minutes, both teams were in place.

"They have a large APC parked just inside the cave," Sergeant Young called over his AN/PRT-4 hand-held radio. "It's manned, but the guards seem pretty lax."

Victor eyed the machine gun nest blocking the entrance of the cave and spoke quietly into his radio. "Wait until we start shooting, then use your LAWs to hit the APC."

"Will do," Young answered. He turned to Zeller and Neal. "Each of you take a LAW and extend it. On my order, we'll hit the APC with all three of the rockets."

The sergeant turned to the translator. "Jaber, tell the Qahidi to wait until after we launch our rockets at the vehicle in the cave. Then they should try to hit anyone offering resistance *provided* it isn't the prince. Be *sure* they know not to shoot the prince."

"I understand," Jaber replied. He quietly explained the orders to the Bedouins.

Lieutenant Victor readied his men hidden near the eastern cave, eyeing the .50 caliber machine gun sitting in its sandbag emplacement with its three-man crew. Five guards sat deeper into the cave, smoking in the darkness as they talked, their AUG rifles resting against the wall of the cave.

The American lieutenant glanced up and down

the line of Delta Force troops, their weapons trained on the cave.

He gave the order: "Fire!"

There were loud plops from the American grenadiers' M203s and an eruption of gunfire from the other weapons. The projectiles from the M203s landed inside the machine gun nest and exploded.

The men in the nest were peppered by the deadly fragments from the grenades and dropped where they were beside the Browning MG. The two Minimi machine guns and M16s cut into the remaining guards struggling to reach their rifles.

The gunfire and explosions signaled Sergeant Young. "Fire," he yelled as Victor's squad charged the eastern cave with guns still blazing in three-round bursts.

At the western cave, Young, Zeller, and Neal ignored the din and kept their rocket launcher sights centered on the APC, using the proper stadia wires for the 40-meter distance from their target. With the order to fire, they removed the weapon's safety and reached for the fire levers.

As they depressed the levers, the turret of the APC rotated toward Lieutenant Victor's squad. The gun in the turret sputtered a short burst that went wide of the charging American soldiers. The gunner was rotating his turret to acquire the proper range when the three LAW rockets erupted from their launch tubes.

The projectiles flew at the APC, hitting it before the gunner could fire his machine gun a second time. The three warheads exploded, their tips sending high-velocity streams of molten steel through the steel plate, killing the crew almost instantly.

The two Bedouins next to Young immediately fired a salvo at the three armed men who came charging from behind the burning APC. The heavy fusillade chewed into the men, who fell to the rocky floor of the cave without firing a shot.

Sergeant Young threw aside his empty fiberglass launch tube, retrieved his carbine as he was standing up and bellowed, "Charge!" over the tumult of gunfire and crackling flames.

The Americans and Bedouins raced to the western cave as a handful of reinforcements emerged from inside, firing through the flames of the burning APC. The reinforcements were cut down by the hail of gunfire from the American and Qahidi weapons.

Lieutenant Victor's squad entered the eastern cave as a band of swordsmen on horseback came charging from the depths of the passageway.

The Delta Force soldiers immediately opened fire on the horsemen. Gunfire, screams, and neighing echoed from the ceiling and walls of the cave prompting Lieutenant Victor to wonder for a fleeting moment if the noise might trigger a cave-in.

The horses and their riders were sliced down by the massive volley from the American weapons. The resulting stench of gunpowder and blood filled the air as Victor and his troops picked their way through the bodies of men and animals.

Many of the Delta Force troops took the opportunity to exchange their nearly expended magazines for full ones during the lull in the fighting. The empty plastic magazines clattered to the floor as the soldiers advanced into the cave.

They charged down the tunnel, dimly lit by a string of lights along the ceiling. The passageway widened into a cavern that had been used as a stable for the horses. The Americans eyed the five camels still tied up in the chamber, and then noticed the heavy steel door to one side of the huge room.

One of the soldiers tried the door handle. "Locked," he told Victor.

The officer gave his order, "Stevens and Gordon, take out that door. The rest of you, stand back. You two," he motioned to another pair of riflemen, "return to the mouth of the tunnel and guard the entrance to the cave so we don't get trapped in here."

Stevens and Gordon sprinted to the steel door, set their rifles down, and removed their back packs. They opened the packs, retrieving clay-like C4 explosives from inside. The two soldiers broke open the containers and molded the material into balls that they slapped onto the steel plate of the door, sticking them next to the heavy hinges and lock.

Next, they inserted electric blasting caps into each mount of C4 stuck to the steel plate. Each man attached a priming adapter and its wires to the cap, then stretched the cables a safe distance to either side of the door.

"Stand clear," Private Gordon warned the other troops as he attached the wires to the 10-cap blasting machine he withdrew from his pack. He swiftly screwed the wires to the twin terminals, then inserted the generator handle that had been hanging on a chain into the shaft of the blasting machine.

"We're ready, Lieutenant Victor," Gordon announced.

"Stand clear!" Victor yelled to his men. "Team one ready with your stun grenades."

He spoke to the demolition experts. "On three."

There was silence, then the lieutenant counted, "One . . . Two . . . Three!"

Gordon twisted the lever on the blasting machine. The C4 exploded, rocking the cavern and blowing the steel door into the room beyond. The entry team raced forward, heaving their flash bang grenades into the chamber, inducing loud explosions with bright blinding light.

Within seconds after the explosions, the entry team dashed into the room, finding Qaim and his sons, along with the prince, lying on the floor, still dazed by the noise and light from the flash bangs. The American soldiers quickly rolled the compliant men onto their faces and secured their hands and legs with plastic quick-lock strips they carried in their vests.

Another team of soldiers raced past and headed down the hallway to check the restroom and bedrooms that lay beyond. Each door was kicked open and a stun grenade heaved in before a soldier entered with his rifle at the ready. Within seconds, all rooms had been searched.

"Secured," one of the soldiers proclaimed as Lieutenant Victor entered the room.

"Good job," the officer congratulated his men. He inspected the five Bedouins sitting on the floor with their hands and feet bound. "You must be Prince Sulaiman," he said.

"Yes, I am and you must let me go," the prince said desperately. "These men have kidnapped me and—"

"Sorry," the officer answered. "We know you're in on it. With any luck we'll have you to your father within the hour."

The prince glared at the soldier and was silent as the thumping of helicopter blades reverberated from outside the cavern.

"We've secured our objective, Desert Hen," Oz reported to Warner over the COMSAT. "How soon can you get the tanker to us? Over."

"I've got bad news, Desert One," Warner responded. "We've lost the tanker somewhere over Algeria. The Pentagon believes it was shot down. Over."

Oz glanced at his watch. "If we had fuel we could still make the deadline. But as it is . . ."

"There must be fuel in the guards' vehicles," Warner suggested.

"That's a negative," Oz answered. "They mostly used animals for travel, and the APC was being used as a fixed position. There might be fuel in some of the V-22s, but they're too far away. We'd be empty before we reached them.

"Hey, wait a minute!" the pilot exclaimed. "Let me check on something. I'll get back to you right away. Over and out."

31

The CCN TV camera zoomed in on the king as he stepped from his limousine, pausing to speak briefly to an official next to the podium.

Stacy Stallworth's voice was fed over the picture beamed into space. "Here's the king now," she reported. "There continues to be speculation that his son may have been released. But our confidential sources—as well as a spokesman for the government—all agree there is no validity to these rumors."

The ruler disappeared for a moment in a crowd of officials and bodyguards, then mounted the steps leading to the podium. There was a brief scuffle to the left of the stage as a soldier mistook a newsman's tiny camera for a weapon. The problem was quickly settled, but not without considerable embarrassment on both sides.

The lenses of scores of cameras turned their cold eyes to the king, who now stood at the podium. There was a squeal of feedback from one poorly adjusted microphone, then both the electrical circuits and the newsmen became silent.

"As you already know," King Khadduri began amid an eruption of camera flashes, "My son has been kidnapped and, I believe, killed. We now have evidence that this abominable crime was committed by a coalition representing the heads of the Qahidi, Sa'adi, and Banu Hilal tribes. These cowardly men exploited the tribal peace conference my son so generously sponsored only to trick us and kill Prince Sulaiman. Only this morning, one of their hired killers was found atop the building across the street, clearly preparing to assassinate me during this very press conference."

The king paused, the distant thumping of helicopter blades distracting him. Then the ruler continued, raising his voice over the growing roar. "It is therefore, with great sorrow, that I declare a war of retribution on the tribes of—"

As the beating of the helicopter blades grew louder, the ruler twirled to see an MH-60K storming toward the open courtyard. He ducked as the black machine hurtled over his head, coming in too low to be detected by East Sahran radar.

"What is this outrage!" Khadduri cried into the mikes. He held onto his *keffiyeh* to keep it from being blown away by the wash from the chopper's blades as it returned to hover over the courtyard.

Newsmen scattered in all directions, clearing an open space as it became obvious the helicopter was slowly dropping to the courtyard. The pilot waited impatiently for the crowd to disperse. Finally, everyone was out from under the MH-60K.

Oz lowered his chopper to the ground, glancing at the nearly full reading of the fuel gauge; the gasoline they'd drained from the electrical generator's tanks was burning perfectly in the MH-60K. The landing gear touched the concrete, crushing two folding chairs as the heavy machine settled.

An honor guard of burly Qahidi tribesmen bounded from the open side door of the helicopter as the news cameras swiveled toward them. A newsman jerked the plug on the public address system into which the king was babbling so they could hear what the Bedouins from the chopper were saying.

The helicopter's engines wound down gradually as Oz and O.T. escorted Prince Sulaiman from the aircraft. The crowd of pushing newsmen shouted questions and shoved their microphones at the three men as an angry King Khadduri stomped off the stage. His son immediately turned and left, following his father.

"Who had the prince?" one of the newsmen yelled.

"The kidnapping was a hoax," Oz answered.

"Did the king know about it?"

"I don't know the answer to that," the pilot said. "Now, if you'll excuse us—"

"The king reported that his son was dead," Stacy Stallworth hollered.

"Obviously Prince Sulaiman is not dead."

The pilot had turned to leave when Stallworth yelled another query, "You're calling the king a liar then?"

"No," Oz replied wearily, turning back to the cameras. "I'm simply saying the prince was in full control of the people who were hiding him."

"Then *you* actually kidnapped him in bringing him here," Stallworth followed up.

Oz thought a moment, aware that the whole world was watching. "The king ordered the prince returned by the deadline. We simply returned him according to the king's demands. Now if you'll excuse me, we need to tend to our wounded."

Oz, O.T., and the Qahidi tribesmen walked back to the helicopter. Before boarding the MH-60K, the pilot shook hands with Abd el Taha Izaak. "I appreciate your help," he said.

Jaber translated for the *qa'id* as Oz continued. "I must return to the salt mine to team up with the other members in my group. But I've talked to my commander and we'll be sending one of the President's new Peace Corp volunteer groups to help rebuild your village and undo the damage we caused by our attack."

Izaak spoke in Arabic as he shook the American pilot's hand.

"Thank you for saving my tribe and my country," Jaber translated.

Oz turned and climbed into his chopper.

E P I L O G U E

Within hours of the return of Prince Sulaiman, the President of the United States ordered a second detachment of Night Stalkers be flown into Morocco. From there, the six helicopters in the second team flew to Bhaliq, where they picked up Sergeant Marvin and his ground crew as well as the remaining Delta Force soldiers.

Next, they journeyed to the desert salt mines to link up with the two remaining aircraft from Oz's team. The eight choppers then returned to Morocco and—after the helicopters had been prepared for shipment in the two C-5As that waited for them—headed for the United States.

One week later, F-14 "Tomcats" from the USS *Nimitz* engaged in a series of bombing runs, penetrating Libyan air space. The American jets destroyed much of the renegade country's air force in what a State Department spokesman termed a "surgical air strike."

"I can't believe it," O.T. said as he, Oz, and Death Song strolled along the brightly-lit hospital hallway, their polished boots clicking on the surface. "You're telling me that just a few hours ago General Mahala took over the government?"

Oz nodded. "The king and his son were arrested. Mahala claims that he'll hold elections in six months. In the meantime, it looks like the general's giving all four Bedouin tribes an equal say in the government. I suspect it'll be touch-and-go as to whether he gives up the reins of power in six months, but at least it seems hopeful."

"Isn't this the room?" Death Song asked, indicating the numerals.

"Yeah," O.T. answered. The warrant officer pushed his way through the wide door, followed by Oz and Death Song.

"Well, look what the cat dragged in," Luger smiled wanly. "You guys look like you've seen better days."

"I bet you haven't been getting much rest around here," O.T. said, raising an eyebrow at the good-looking nurse checking the digital thermometer.

"If I had a nurse like you," Death Song grinned, "I'd try never to get well."

"If she had a patient like you," Luger smiled, "she'd be looking for another line of work."

"Don't stay too long, *gentlemen,*" the nurse smirked. "He isn't in perfect health—yet!"

Duncan Long is internationally recognized as a firearms expert, and has had over twenty books published on that subject, as well as numerous magazine articles. In addition to his nonfiction writing, Long has written a science fiction novel, *Antigrav Unlimited*. He has an M.A. in music composition, has worked as a rock musician and he has spent nine years teaching in public schools. Duncan Long lives in eastern Kansas with his wife and two children.

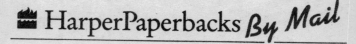